Early Bird Writers Group Presents...

David 2

False realities expressed every day!

F.R.E.E

Preston A. Dent

**Pennsylvania Canada D.C London Tokyo
Australia**

Africa New York Atlanta Kansas City Abu Dhabi

California Miami Texas Chicago

Dubai Paris Puerto Rico

World Wide

HEAD OF THE SNAKE

v

My Dedication

First and foremost, I would like to dedicate this novel to my lord and savior, for him giving me strength and the imagination. My three son's Preston, Princeton, Pierceton, and the ones in my family that believe in me. To everyone who helped this project become a success, my editors, proof reader's, PR's, and critics. I want to say thank you to my Early Bird Writers Group partner Samira. I dedicate this book to anyone who made a change for the better. To those who sacrificed right or wrong to feed their family. This story is dedicated to every son and daughter who lost somebody to this treacherous game. To every innocent bystander caught in a shootout, losing their life to a bullet that wasn't theirs. To the families of the inmates sending letters, visiting, and putting money on their loved ones commissary. To the people who were gunned down, assaulted, and dying by the hands of the police. To the ones before me who fought for our rights, freedom, trying to show that black lives matter.

The boy from under

a Rock

THE heart of a thousand kings, the blood of a thousand slaves. He danced with growling wolves and he walked with roaring lions. He was a soldier through any price, burden, opposing any foe to assure his survival. David was born with less, without a silver spoon or a lucky four leaf clover. The telephone was empty that he talked through. The hallways were empty that he walked through. David grew to be a stranger to love, to happiness, never being in position to enjoy the joys of life. David wasn't given a choice, an option, he was forced to play cards dealt by a demon. From his mother dying in a prison to being forced into the life of sorrow. His foster father molested him, abused him, making him smoke *"Crack Cocaine"* the devils potion. David was the boy from under a rock that cried, prayed, and wished the pain stopped.

SHADOW AS A FRIEND

Poem by Preston A. Dent

HE NEVER SHOWED A SMILE, NOT
EVEN A GRIN,

ALL THE KIDS TEASED HIM FOR
THE COLOR OF HIS SKIN.

LONELY IN THIS WORLD, HE WAS
BORN TO SIN,

WALKING, HEAD DOWN, WITH A

SHADOW AS A FRIEND.

WITH NONE TO GUIDE HIM
THROUGH HIS ENDEAVORS,

HE GREW VIOLENTLY, FOLDING
FROM LIFE'S PRESSURES,

FALSE REALITIES EXPRESSED
EVERY DAY

NO LECTURES,

THE BOY FROM UNDER A ROCK,
SATANS MESSENGER!

CHAPTER 1

LAST 2 STAND

Treasures of War

The surface of the earth. One could hear the squirrels playing as they raced through the trees. The birds chirped and hovered above as they synchronized in circular formations. The lifeless bodies of the dead soldiers, who fought with honor, lay sprawled on the ground. One can only pray their souls went to Heaven. The aroma of death was foul, unpleasant, and reminiscent of a battlefield. The Earth was covered with bullet casings, blood, and corpses. The police sirens could be heard echoing from blocks away, becoming louder by the second. The air was silent—no movements, noises, and everything was still. Everything except one thing; one thing our creator intended to be heard. There was a pulse, a heartbeat, the spark of a boy from under a rock. A deep rose of blackness with razor sharp thorns on the stem breaking through the concrete and soil.

He slowly rose up and shook his head, opening both of his eyes. His vision was blurry, fuzzy—barely there. Looking left to right, he realized he was the last man alive. He tried to stand, but tumbled to one knee. He took a deep breath and then stood with wobbly legs. As he heard the police sirens closing in upon him with no time to think, he grabbed his guns and put them back into his duffle bag. He slung the bag over his shoulder and vanished through the alleyway. Slowly gaining his strength, he recognized sharp pains coming from his back. He had two bullets lodged in the back of his bullet proof vest that had knocked him out cold.

David continued running on foot, thanking God that he had survived the battle. He noticed a civilian running behind him telling him to stop.

David thought to himself, *What the fuck is wrong with this nut ass dude, I'm about to take his life away!*

The civilian was an older white man in his late thirties; a pretty fast runner catching up to David quickly. He grabbed the back of David's hoodie in an attempt to apprehend him. David turned around and

2

pistol whipped him with the barrel of his gun. He swung the gun with all of his might, and by the expression on David's face, it was clear to see that he wasn't to be fucked with. The man lifted his arm as if he were trying to defend himself.

David put the gun to the middle of the man's head.

The white guy spoke in a teary voice, *"No—No, please, please I'm begging don't shoot. My mother is sick and I have twins on the way."*

David was coldhearted, abiding by his lifetime rule of *dead people don't talk and live witnesses are critical.* He knew that the cops were closing in and didn't want them to know his direction. David had a split second to think, knowing that the man would give the police his description. David thought for that second and made up his mind, *fuck it,* and squeezed the trigger. The man's face split in half while particles of his brain flew away. David grabbed the bottom of his shirt and wiped the splattered blood off his face.

He continued running as if nothing ever happened. At this point, killing was second nature to him; every murder was becoming easier. David knew there was no turning back now, so first thing he had to do was get rid of his guns.

He was running out of energy fast; sweating and trying to catch his breath. He had no idea of his location; all he knew is that he was in York, Pennsylvania. The neighborhood was ghostly, with a few abandoned apartment buildings, and crime watch signs all over the neighborhood.

David hid behind an unoccupied house to get his thoughts together. He bent over, dropping the duffle bag beside him, and tightened the laces on his black timberlands. Taking a deep breath, he then cleared his nasal passage, spitting the phlegm onto the floor. David had to figure something out; he knew the whole force would be searching the area. They would block off every road and search every house. They would have the K-9 dogs sniffing for trails and helicopters as the eyes in the sky.

As David caught his breath he was ready to proceed. After he relieved himself of the evidence he carried inside his duffle bag, he would then set out to get his pregnant girlfriend. The thoughts of freedom infiltrated his mind giving him God-willing strength, the will to push to the maximum. David peeked around the alley wall, trying not to be spotted as he watched the area. Inching his body closer with one eye peeking, he tried to see if the coast was clear. On the left, he glimpsed a gray house with its garage door open.

There were two vehicles inside, one a silver Camry and the other a black Tahoe.

David thought, *I'm hopping in that Tahoe and getting low.* Grabbing the duffle bag with little time to think, he reluctantly darted toward the garage. Through his peripheral vision, he made sure there weren't any wandering eyes. He tried to open the back door of the truck but it was locked.

David squatted low to the ground, checking all of the doors of the truck. All the doors were locked except for the driver's side. He smiled while opening it quietly. He climbed inside of the Tahoe and laid down on the back seat thinking to himself, *I'm going to sit here till the coast is clear. Anybody step foot in this garage will meet they maker.*

A half hour passed with no sounds of helicopters, no cop sirens, and the owners of the house hadn't made themselves present. David sat there patiently, thinking about the situation that just occurred; flashes of the war, the cops, of King escaping by the skin of his teeth. David was agitated, angry thinking, *I had that motherfucker in the palm of my hands.*

Three hours passed; they were the longest three hours of his life. The whole time he contemplated what should or would he do if the cops found him? *Should I go out blasting and shoot my way out, or give up and fight it at trial?* David figured that the coast was clear, but just as he was in preparation to exit, he heard a vehicle pull up. David laid back down on the seat of the truck praying it wasn't the police.

Then he heard their scanners and walkie talkies. *"Fuck. Fuck. Fuck."* The garage was pitch black, so when the cops shined their flashlights they appeared as bright as the moon. The cops hoped they would see someone or anything that looked suspicious. The owner turned the lights on when he realized that there was a cop car outside of his house.

"Is there something I can help you with, officer?" the owner asked.

"You just might, sir. There was a big shootout between gangs and police officers. You wouldn't happen to have seen anything suspicious now, would you?"

"What do you mean, suspicious?" the owner said with an attitude.

"A couple buddies of mine, good Samaritan cops, were murdered in cold blood," the officer replied hastily.

"I am sorry to hear that, sir, but I haven't heard or seen anything suspicious. You officers have a nice day."

The police car drove away, still searching the area high and low; the city of York was in an uproar. The news, radio, streets, and social media were all talking about it. David watched the owner tie a knot in the trash bag and carry it to the curb.

He came back inside and started walking toward the garage switch. "Oh shit! I knew I had to come out here for something."

He turned around and walked back toward the Tahoe, opened the driver's side door, then started searching through the middle console. The owner found what he was looking for—a white envelope. He put it in his back pocket, never even realizing that David was lying in the back seat. *Imagine sitting there, heart beating faster and faster, stomach full of butterflies, praying not to be spotted.*

David was trying his hardest not to make a sound. Thinking, *Fuck it, if it goes down, this pussy's taking me to freedom or I'm poppin' his ass.*

As the owner finished placing the unneeded items back into the console, he got out of the car and shut the door. He walked toward the back of the Tahoe, trying to look through the dark tinted windows. Something felt strange and out of the ordinary; the owner knew something was fishy and he could smell the tartar sauce. David slowly lifted his gun, pointing it in preparation to open fire. The owner put his face to the window to look through it again, then opened up the door.

"What the hell? What you doing in my truck, motherfucker?" the owner snapped.

David pointed the black and grey 40 Cal that he took from Smalls and pointed it to the man's face. "Shut the fuck up and relax, this isn't a robbery, I'm not coming to kill you. Listen to what I say bra and you will make it home to see your wife and kids before dinner."

The owner of the house calmed down as much as possible, realizing the odds were against him. He knew David could want only one or two things: money or a ride. He went to open the door as if he was getting ready to hop in the driver seat.

"What the fuck you doing, my boy? Climb your ass through the passenger seat and don't try to be a hero. Play Superman and end up super dead, you hear me?"

The owner respected and obeyed David's command, climbing in through the passenger side and hopping into the driver's seat. He put the key in the ignition, put the car in reverse, fixed the mirror, and backed out of the garage. The owner drove down the street and pulled up to a stop sign. An old white lady with a golden retriever was waiting to cross the street. The owner was still nervous; he signaled for the lady to go past them. David showed a smile, waving so she wouldn't think anything was out of the ordinary.

The owner spoke, "So what you want from me, man?"

"Bra, I need to get the fuck low. Feel me?" David said

"So I take it those cops were after you?"

"Yeah, they on my top heavy. Nothing against you, bra. I just want to be free," David said.

After driving for fifteen minutes, David started strategizing his next move, thinking about where he should go. He knew that with nobody to trust, this was going to be a long and frustrating journey.

Every human being appeared to be the police and it was driving David crazy. The whole drive David had the 40 Cal pointed to the left side of the man's rib cage. The man, who appeared to be in his early forties, had dark skin and stood at about about 5'10" 190 pounds. He had a Philadelphia baseball cap on, so his hair style was covered. His facial hair was neat, as if he just got a line up, wearing a full beard that looked like Rick Ross'. Through David's mind, there were racing thoughts; thoughts of the victims he slaughtered,

9

thoughts of Danielle and the baby. David started to become frustrated, telling the owner, "Make a left on George Street."

The owner of the Tahoe remained quiet, obeying his orders. He put his turn signal on and turned onto George Street, waiting for his next instruction. David had never been under this type of pressure before; everything he did had a calculated plan. The owner kept driving, still waiting for David to say something.

David was looking left to right, right to left, looking for a good spot to pull over. He finally saw a low-key parking space in this alleyway. When David went to turn back around, he turned right into the barrel of a 357 snub nose pointed directly at his temple. It was chrome with a rose wood handle similar to the one Clint Eastwood had in his movie *Dirty Harry*.

"Look, young brother, I care nothing about that cop shit. I hold no loyalty to the pigs. I'm from the streets myself. You're in my truck, hiding in my garage, and got your pistol drawn on me on some crazy shit."

The look on David's face was of surprise. He always had the upper hand; always had the first strike. The owner still had the chrome 357 to David's face. With the other hand, he took David's gun and put it in his glove compartment. The whole time he stared David in the eye, watching his every move. The owner held the gun firm, with his finger on the trigger, as if he wanted to squeeze. The owner thought to himself, *this is only a boy*. The owner was at a point in his life that he had a few things lined up. His business was good, and his family was happy and well. Deep inside his soul he didn't want to take David's life. So instead of killing him, he decided to give him some words of wisdom.

"Look, dawg, take this here as a message. Know that there is a God, and he had to have heard your prayers tonight. I could turn you in, or I could paint my Tahoe red with your brains. I've been there before, so I understand the struggle. I'd rather feed you game that will get you ahead, lil bra. Clean your life up and get focused, dawg. These streets is one way in and no way out."

David was shocked by his response, knowing he had to be knowledgeable of the game. He said some real ass shit, leaving him no choice but to respect it!

"Thanks, bra. I see I'm not the only real nigga left." David nodded his head to the owner and put his hood over his head. The owner nodded back, reaching inside of the glove compartment to grab David's gun. He took a cloth from the backseat and carefully wiped off his finger prints before giving the gun back to David.

"Never lose faith in GOD, bra, and he will guide you through your endeavors."

He shook the man's hand and hopped out of the truck. David looked at him one last time to make sure he remembered the man's face and fled into the darkness.

CHAPTER 2

GREAT ESCAPE

Hard to Kill

avid left the black Tahoe thankful that the old head didn't take his life. He accepted his blessings as if it was a sign from God, thinking he was on this earth for a purpose. David was making his way to the inner city toward Danielle's house. He was walking, yet creeping through the shadows of the city's alleyways. The sky was hungry, sounding like an empty belly, as thunder rumbled the air waves. David sighed as he stared above him, watching the clouds form in preparation to release rain. The wind was blowing, knocking around trash cans and empty gallons of juice containers. The stray cats, skunks, all ran and took cover. The alley was covered with drug paraphernalia, orange needle lids, broken antennas, and empty baggies everywhere. The weather, on the other hand, was working on David's behalf. Rain was a perfect camouflage. There wouldn't be anyone outside—no nosey neighbors or little kids playing and running around. David thought, *I might as well take apart these guns.* David stood inside of an abandoned garage. There was nothing inside except piles of blunt guts and black oil that leaked from whatever car that was there prior.

David dropped his duffle bag and unzipped it, pulling both murder weapons out. He first grabbed the 40 Cal that he took from Smalls and then grabbed the sawed off shotgun he killed Smooth with. He put his black gloves on and, taking the bottom of his shirt, and started wiping off both of the weapons. He carefully made sure his finger prints were thoroughly removed. When he finished taking both of the guns apart, he put all of the pieces in a plastic bag he found in the alley. David left the duffle bag and started walking out of the garage. The rain was coming down vigorously, quickly soaking David's attire. David embraced the rain drops, the earth's showers, understanding that when it rains it pours. Thinking that when it rained it was God crying out to his children on earth.

David continued walking through the alley. Every two blocks he would hide a piece of the gun. He untied the knot to a trash bag that was in a green trash can and put two pieces of the gun inside of it. He did the same thing until all of the pieces were gone. The trash men would come behind him and empty all of the trash cans, so this was the perfect idea. David got rid of all the evidence thinking, *now all I have to do is get to Danielle's house safely!* He had an extra gun hidden, buried deep under the grass in her back yard. He also had to get his six grand and jewelry, because he had no idea as to what Danielle's state of mind was toward him. He couldn't afford any losses nor take any chances. It wasn't Danielle that he didn't trust—it was her mother!

After walking for an hour, David became antsy as he got closer to Danielle's house. He decided it best to change his identity, but he didn't have enough money on him to buy a new outfit. All he had was enough to get a haircut. So while David was walking, he started taking out all of his braids so he could just walk straight in the barber shop. Hopefully a barber shop was in the direction he was going. The storm had died down and David was soaked from the rain. He came around the corner with his hoodie over his head and noticed a plaza with multiple businesses. There was a barber shop, an arcade, a soul food restaurant, and Mid K—a beauty supply store that was run by Hindu's. David was more paranoid than ever, not having any idea as to who may have known his identity.

So David took his hoodie off and opened the door of the barber shop, which was right in the center of the complex. The shop had six chairs, but only four male barbers, an older man with a gray beard, a heavyset guy with dreads, one tatted up with body piercings, and the other was short with a blond and red Mohawk. The other two chairs were occupied by one female and one Male. The female was threading eyebrows and the guy was shampooing a client's hair. David had never seen a barber shop like this, thinking, *this shit is weird as fuck, bra.*

"How many heads you have left?" David said to the older man.

"You're next, young man. Give me ten minutes and you're right in."

"Cool, good looking."

The older man had finally finished cutting his client's hair. David looked at the person whose hair he had just cut, making sure that his hair cutting skills was official. The man sprayed alcohol over the Sanex neck strip and started patting it over his client's face and neck. He wiped all of the hair off of the black cape and took it off of his client. His client looked in the mirror smiling, impressed, and thanked the barber for his expertise.

"I'm ready for you, young man. What can I do for you today?"

"I'm tired of these braids, man. I need a new look, so just give me an even one all over and follow my natural line," David said

"No problem. I'm going to take care of you, my brother."

The barber combed through David's hair with one hand and with the other he used a pair of scissors. He was trying to get David's hair as low as possible to make it easier for the clippers to go through.

"Do you want me to use the razor or is it cool the way it is?" the barber asked.

David looked in the mirror, looking side to side; making sure the barber didn't do him wrong. David was pleased, enjoying his new look. His lineup was shitty sharp like Lil josh did it. David hated razors and would never let someone put it to his face, thinking everyone wanted him dead and out da game.

"Okay, OG. I see you nice with them clippers. Nah, this straight, bra, good

looking."

The barber didn't have a cocky or arrogant personality; he was modest, more sure of his talented art. All of the barbers in the shop were checking out David's new haircut; his good grade of hair made it dark and crisp like a GQ model.

"Damn boy, how old are you? I might have to get my R Kelly on," the female hairstylist said.

"Hussy, he ain't worried about you. He need a bitch like me," the gay guy snapped.

Everybody in the Barber shop started laughing, but David didn't take kindly to what the gay guy said.

"What the fuck you just say? I don't play them type of games, bra. I ain't one of them niccaz," David said frowning.

Before David could say anything else, one of the other barbers stepped in front of David. "They just joking with you. They mean you no harm or disrespect"

"Nah, bra, I don't have nothing against gay folks. Just don't be playing with me like that, you feel me?" David said.

David reached in his pocket and pulled out a twenty dollar bill and handed it to the Barber. The barber handed him back a ten dollar bill and told him thanks for his business. "You come on back and see us again, my friend. Take care." After David took care of his identity, there was only one thing left to do now. Call Danielle.

CHAPTER 3

PHONE CALL

You never know

David reached in his pocket and grabbed two quarters, and after the second one slipped into the slot of the pay phone he dialed Danielle's phone number. He had no idea what she would say, how she would say it, or what she knew. He stood there jittery, nervous, as the phone rang hoping.

"Hello hello? Who is this?" Danielle said. David sat there silently, mute and scared to speak.

"Hello! Whoever this is, stop playing on my phone please!" Danielle said. *Click*! David was torn with emotion knowing that he had to show face and explain himself. He was getting ready to call her back, but quickly realized he didn't have any more change. David was a wanted man with no financial resources outside of what Danielle held. He had no other choice but to compromise with the situation regardless of what she knew. He walked inside of the corner store to get change. He handed the clerk a dollar bill and asked for four quarters. The clerk told him that he must first buy something; he was being a complete asshole. That's all David had left in his pocket was a dollar and a ten dollar bill. He only needed fifty cents to call Danielle and another fifty cents to call a cab to her house. He was not in the mood for anyone's bullshit.

"See, this how motherfuckers commit suicide. All I wanted was some damn change! Normally, I would pull my gun out, smack you with it, and then take everything. Matter a fact, I should leave your fat funky ass stinking like a pig with two holes in your head, pussy!"

The clerk smirked, sucking his teeth, and mumbled beneath his breath sarcastically. He quickly changed his mindset, realizing that David wasn't the average customer. He took the dollar bill and gave David the change, and then looked at the door for David to leave. David snapped out and smacked all of the items off of the counter. He kicked over the chip and nutty bar stand before walking out of the store, sticking up his middle finger. *Fucking nut ass dude.*

David walked back to the payphone. As he approached, he noticed someone was on it. He sat there for thirty seconds waiting for them to get off the phone. The person was engulfed in a conversation, joking and laughing, as if he didn't have a care in the world. David was pressed for time and was beginning to get very impatient. He started approaching the person, ready to make them get off of the phone. As soon as he got close, a police car drove past with two Caucasian cops inside. David kept his head down and walked past the payphone, trying not to be obvious while hiding his face. He prepared himself to flee; not wanting to take a chance, but the cops paid him no attention and kept driving down the street. He turned back around to make the white dude get off of the phone, but he was already gone. David took the phone off the hook and put the quarters inside of the coin slot.

"The prettiest girl in the world. I haven't heard my baby voice in a minute. What it do? Baby, I miss you."

"David! Oh my God! I thought that you were dead."

"Hell nah, I'm not dead. Why would you think that? Girl, don't be wishing no death on me. You tripping!" David said

"Me and my mom seen the news, that's what they've been saying all day."

Before she could finish her sentence, David quickly cut her off. "Baby, you going crazy, you know I don't talk like that over these phones. Aye, we gonna talk in person. Get my stuff together and I'm coming to pick you up."

"Yes, because we really need to talk. So how long will it be before you get here? And make sure you pull around back, because my mother is home and you know she's not your biggest fan right now."

"Oh yeah?"

"It's cool though. Give me twenty minutes, boo I'll be there."

"Okay," Danielle said.

Danielle hung up the phone with all sorts of mixed emotions inside of her pregnant body. She was trying her hardest not to break down and release saddened tears from her innocent glands. She was sitting in the front room resting her feet. The couches were suede with fluffy pillows specifically for comfort.

She picked up the remote control and turned off the T.V, the cable box and the space heater plugged into her wall. Danielle didn't know whether to be afraid or happy—all she knew was that the man of her dreams was on his way to pick her up. Danielle got off of the couch and started walking up the stairs. She held onto the rail as she suddenly became light headed. Taking a breath, she continued, knowing David would be there in twenty minutes. Danielle made it up the stairs and headed toward her bedroom.

"Danielle, did you see the cordless phone," Danielle's mother asked.

"It's downstairs in the living room on the couch, mom."

"Okay, what are you about to do? Did you call your father back?

"No, not yet mom, but I'm going to call him a little later."

"Okay, make sure that you do because he's coming back from Europe in three weeks and he said he hasn't talked to you in months," Danielle's mother said.

"Okay, mom, I'm going to make sure I call him."

Danielle opened up her room door and walked inside. She grabbed David's money, jewels, and the rest of his belongings and put them in a grey and maroon Nike book bag. She got all of his things together and patiently waited for David's arrival. Then the phone rang.

"Hello."

"It's me. I'm out back. And don't forget to grab a few outfits and whatever else you need because we getting a room for a couple days."

"Okay, I already got my stuff together. Boy, you act like I'm slow. I got to think of something to tell my mom now," Danielle said.

"Why you say that?"

"David, I told you my mom seen the news and the things that they were saying about you."

"Well, just tell her you going over your home girl's or something," David said.

"My mom is not stupid."

Danielle and David had no idea that Danielle's mother was listening to their entire phone conversation.

"You damn right I am not stupid. And, Danielle, you're not going anywhere with him! No, No, Danielle! He is trouble! You heard what the news said."

Danielle's mother loved her with all of her heart and would protect her by any means necessary. "Why are you listening to my phone conversation? I swear I have no privacy in this house." David sat there quietly not saying a word, waiting for an opportunity to say that he was outside.

"If you coming, I'm out here, Danielle, and to you, Ms. Bradshaw, I'm sorry that you feel that way. If I had a dollar for every time I heard a rumor about me, I would be a millionaire." Then he hung up the phone.

Danielle ran back downstairs looking for her mother. She was pissed off.

"Mom, why would you do that? I am not a little kid anymore."

"I don't care what you say; you're not leaving with him. I will not allow you to do this to yourself. They are saying that he is a murderer, that he has HIV. Come on, Danielle, you can't be that stupid. I raised you smarter than this."

"Mom, all I'm doing is going to find out what is going on. Trust me; I know what I'm doing."

Danielle's mother was stubborn, thick headed, and wasn't trying to understand one word that was coming out of Danielle's mouth. She stood in front of the door spreading out her arms, trying to block the door. The phone started ringing; Danielle looked at the caller I.D. seeing that it was David. He couldn't sit around too long and was rushing her to come on. Danielle tried to grab the phone, but her mother wouldn't give it to her.

"Fine! I am leaving mom. I don't have time or the energy," Danielle uttered as she cried.

Danielle grabbed their belongings and, with what little strength she had left, she stormed past her mother using all of her force. Her mother tried mercilessly to hold on to her, grabbing her arm, but lost her grip. She fell back onto the table making the lamp, portraits, and vase fall onto the floor. Danielle stormed out of the house in tears, slamming the screen door behind her. She walked down the wooden steps and got inside the yellow cab where her man awaited. She gave David a kiss and a hug, and handed him his belongings. Danielle sat there soundlessly with a face full of frustration. Her body was filled with language that spoke anger and rage like someone had gotten her dander up. David had never seen his angel in this temperament. He never saw her peeved.

David wasn't ready to face her; he wasn't ready to tell her everything. He sat there in silence as he grabbed his money from the bag and started counting it. Danielle's mother frantically came running out of the house with one shoe on crying, screaming, and banging on the window of the cab.

"Danielle! Danielle! Stop this, please! What are you doing? You're making a huge mistake."

David told the cab driver to pull off and head toward the hotel.

Danielle's mother put both of her hands to her face and ran inside of the house crying. She paced back and forth trying to get her thoughts together. She didn't know what to do. The first thing that came to her mind was Danielle's father. She desperately started searching for the phone, flipping over pillows, looking on the kitchen counter until she realized it was on top of the T.V. She picked the phone up and dialed Danielle's father's cell phone number. When it went straight to voicemail, she hung the phone up and then tried to call again. He finally answered.

"Hey, there better be a good God damn reason that you're blowing my phone up like this!" Danielle's father said.

Danielle's mother fell into uncontrollable sobbing, incapable of holding her tears back any longer. She tried to compose herself, sniffling,

"Danielle is pregnant by a guy that was on the news. He's wanted for murder, and they're saying he has HIV."

"What? What the hell are you talking about?

"She just left with him and I'm scared. I don't know what else to do."

"So you're telling me that my angel is pregnant and y'all never told me anything? And it's to a guy with AIDS?" Danielle's father snapped.

Danielle's mother burst into tears again. "Yes, yes, you know that I wouldn't lie to you about something like this. Please come, Devon, I need you here with me. I think I'm going to lose my mind."

"When I get there, I swear to God I'm going to stick my foot up some asses." And he hung up the phone.

Meanwhile, David and Danielle were sitting there silent. Neither one of them said a word. "Take us to the Black Roof Inn, my boy," David said. The driver nodded his head and continued heading toward the direction of the hotel.

CHAPTER 4

BLACK ROOF

Lies never end

They made it to the Black Roof Inn in approximately ten minutes. David decided to lay their heads at the Black Roof Inn because of the convenience. All of the other hotels wanted credit cards, ID, and a bunch of other shit.

David looked at the taxi meter seeing that it was 17 dollars. He handed the taxi driver a crisp twenty dollar bill telling him, *"Keep the change, pimp."* David grabbed his belongings, opened the door of the cab, and got out. He shut the door quickly, walking to the other side of the cab to help let Danielle out.

"Come on, baby, let's go."

David reached to help her get out of the cab. David couldn't wait to get inside of the hotel, he was trying his hardest to hide his paranoia. Looking side to side and over his shoulder every second didn't help the situation. David walked to the door, opening it for Danielle. He was being a perfect gentleman. They both walked through the door holding each other's hands, heading toward the check-in desk.

"Damn, not one of these speaks English. Egg roll eating-motherfuckers." The desk clerk was a taller Asian man with glasses and bad breath. His teeth were spaced apart and the front ones were bucked like Roger Rabbit's.

"Do you have any rooms available?" David said.

"Would you like one bed, two bed?"

"Let me get two bed," David said in a high pitched Asian accent that sent Danielle bursting into tears.

"Okay, let me check. For who and can see I your I.D.?"

David kept a couple identification cards for situations like this. Every time he robbed someone, he would keep their I.D. if they looked similar.

"Here you go," David handed him his I.D. and the clerk barely even looked at it. He scanned it and gave it back.

"Room is fifty-six dollar, but with tax seventy-two altogether."

"Alright that's cool," David said.

"Here go, buddy, enjoy yourself. I see you two expecting soon? She look like she having twins," the clerk said jokingly and handed them two keys.

They got on the elevator, both of them still in silence, dreading the inevitable. Danielle had so many questions that needed to be answered. The hotel only had two floors, so their time on the elevator was short. They started walking down the hall, both of them noticing an aroma. They both looked at each other, laughing as the aroma of marijuana was present and very pungent in the air.

David stuck the key inside of the door. Danielle walked in first, checking, inspecting, making sure she was satisfied with the room's sanctuary. David shut the door and put all of his things inside of the closet. He sat down on the bed and kicked off his shoes, then grabbed the remote and turned on the T.V. He started clicking through the channels to see if he could find the news. The room was brisk, chilly, and they could feel the goose bumps rising on their skin.

Danielle hated being cold and turned the heat on so she could relax and get comfortable. She stared, waiting, giving David a look that he knew all so well. She had many questions to ask. No matter how much she wished, how much she longed for this moment, it was becoming an annoying nightmare. She was becoming angry, frustrated. She hated for someone to not pay her attention.

"David, are you going to tell me what the fuck is going on? Why are you sitting over there being all quiet? Why is the news saying this about you? They are saying that you are wanted for murder, that you have HIV."

"What the fuck you mean, bae? I don't know why they said that shit—motherfuckers say anything nowadays. I haven't killed anybody and I definitely don't have AIDs. Bra, they better get the fuck out of here with that nut ass shit!"

Danielle broke into tears, not knowing what to think. She didn't want to believe it to begin with, so naturally she didn't. Danielle just couldn't come to grips that David could have been that type of person—to her he was perfect!

"Baby, I am sorry that I doubted you. I just needed to hear you say it. I knew that you couldn't have done those things and I never really believed them," Danielle said

David stood up out of his seat. He looked deeply into her hypnotizing hazel eyes and wrapped her in his arms. "I would never hurt you. I would never hurt anybody unless I had to. I want to take you places that you have never seen; that's the life I desire for you. If I could put the world in a box and give it to you as a gift, I would. You can never believe the news or the prejudice motherfuckers in the Burg."

David was still witty and able to charm his way out of any situation. He hated the fact that he had to lie to Danielle. Most of all he hated that it was a strong possibility that his girlfriend and child could be infected with HIV. David couldn't tell her the truth—it was far too soon. It wasn't time for the truth to be spoken. David laid down on the bed quietly; he was upset that he put Danielle and the baby in this situation. She was pure, innocent, worthy of a queen and most of all he took her virginity.

David drifted off into deep thought thinking about every life that he took, every girl he had unprotected sex with. The feeling was overwhelming and he couldn't stop the tears that desperately needed to escape. He had no choice but to cry his heart out till Danielle came to console him.

"David, I know something is wrong I can feel it, I am in love with you. You can talk to me about anything. Anything," Danielle said.

"Is that right? Are you sure that you want to hear the life of David? Are you sure that you can handle it? Baby, I don't think you want to ride that roller coaster," David said seriously.

"We have nothing but time. I'm all ears," Danielle said.

"Do you know what it feels like to never have had a mother, father, or a family? My whole life I been told I was a burden. I smile to hide the frowns. I been having nightmares since I can remember, and it's the same demon that's been haunting me. I am tired of this hypocritical life. I am tired of prayers that are never heard or answered. Why did GOD pick me? Why me, what the fuck did I do to deserve this, tell me what the fuck I did? I been molested, born in a fucking prison, forced to smoke crack cocaine at the age of ten. I been through hell and back. My own brother disowned me. I'm nothing to this life I'm just the dirt beneath a shoe, the kid who wasn't good enough to have a family."

David went into to a frenzy snapping out trying to control his rage; he was too close to the edge. David was losing his composure getting angrier by the second. He was so deep in the depths of fire, easily forgetting that Danielle was present. Danielle sat there confused, crying, and frightened, holding her blanket and rocking back and forth. She had never been in a situation like this and didn't know what to do or what to say.

David pulled out his gun and said, "Is this what the world wants? Is this what you want from me? My Lord, are you telling me that you gave up on me? Haven't I suffered enough? Fuck it then. I should put the gun to my head and pull the trigger. Then the world will be better off."

David put the gun to his head and closed his eyes as tears streamed down his cheeks. The barrel dug into the side of his temple. Danielle ran over to him. "No, no. Oh my God, David, please stop this. You are scaring me!" She tried reaching her hand out to take the gun. "David, why are you doing this, I need you, we need you. What about our baby?" Danielle said.

Danielle wasn't strong enough to take the gun from David, and she didn't want to accidentally make him pull the trigger, so she backed off. David was standing there shaking, trembling, and sweating with his eyes shut tightly.

"Baby, I tried and tried to hold my head above them waters, but I'm not strong enough! Danielle, I love you girl. Forever remember me and tell my child about my story, so hopefully she take a different route. I'm sorry, baby."

David opened his eyes to have one last look at his angel, one last look at life. Flashes of his life stormed through his mind a hundred miles a second. David was suddenly feeling relieved as his finger gripped the pearl thin trigger. He took a deep breath, quenched his eyes and pulled the trigger. David squeezed the trigger three times before realizing that there weren't any bullets in the gun. He took out the clip and looked up at Danielle, not knowing that she had taken the bullets out.

He took a deep breath and wiped off his face. His fingers trembled as he laid the gun on top of the counter. Danielle took a deep breath, thanking God she'd taken all of the bullets out of the gun. She was shaken up; she had never seen David do anything like this before.

"Oh my God, you scared the living shit out of me. What the fuck was that about, David?"

"Look, I'm just tired of going through this shit. I have nobody, no family; my father and mother are both dead! Don't you understand that? I been alone my whole life and anybody I did have turned their back on me."

David never intended for his angel to see him all the way in his bag, to see him going crazy, but he had to get it out. He couldn't hide it anymore and needed for her to see his past. From using drugs, foster care, being molested and born in prison. Danielle never knew that David was dealing with such sorrow; never in a million years would she think he'd been through what he had. Even though Danielle said she would understand and accept anything he told her, when David told her his life's trials, naturally she looked at him differently. Danielle was confused, thinking, *what the hell I have got myself into?*

"So, what are you going to do? They are searching high and low for you. I don't want you to turn yourself in until you have your lawyer."

"Absolutely, I'm not turning myself in until I get a lawyer. Fuck them!"

Danielle's mind was puzzled the more knowledgeable she became of David's situations. She was happy he didn't confirm that he had HIV, though she didn't want to believe it anyway. If David would have killed himself in front of her, she would have no longer been human. She smiled with relief, happy that David was alive. And no matter what happened from this day forward, they would handle it together.

As the night's events began to tether down, Danielle and David shifted their conversation toward the baby.

Danielle mentioned to David that she had gone to the doctors for a physical. She assured him nothing was wrong with the baby, she just needed to get a checkup for her weight, blood pressure, height, and vital signs. Her mother highly insisted that the first thing she get was an HIV test. Danielle was still awaiting her results, but they hadn't come back yet. When she told David about getting checked out and that the results were still pending, David's stomach instantly started bubbling.

Fuck. Fuck. Fuck. Oh shit, she's going to find out.

CHAPTER 5

THUGZ LOVE

One last dance

Their hotel room was newly renovated with a thirty-two inch flat screen, a microwave, and a security box to lock up personal things. David was in dire need of a blunt of exotic marijuana; he hadn't smoked in two days. He grabbed the Vanilla Dutch master and licked down the middle of it with his tongue, then used the tip of his two fingers and split it down the middle. David's roll game was perfecto; he always rolled the Dutch perfectly. After David finished rolling the blunt, he grabbed a white towel and soaked it with water. David placed it neatly at the bottom of the door so no one could smell the aroma. He hadn't slept, showered, or eaten in two days. David was getting ready to spark up, but figured it would be better to hop in the shower first. Normally, David would be all over Danielle, sucking and kissing every muscle of her body. He had a million things speeding through his mind, from being infected with HIV to running from the law.

Danielle had every intention of getting up and walking away. After witnessing David trying to commit suicide, she knew she was in a lane she wasn't ready to drive in. The love in her heart was innocent, pure, and being loyal to her man made it hard to walk away. Every memory they shared flashed across her mind like a comet in the sky. She couldn't understand why David never told her about his past. She started shaking her head.

"What's the matter? Oh, it's like that now, you acting all funny and shit? That's fucked up. And you wonder why I never told you," David said.

"No, no, no, David. That's where you're wrong. I am by your side no matter what. I love you with every inch of my heart, and you're the father of my child. I will never leave your side and I accept you for who you are. All I ask is that you understand where I'm coming from. I'm worried about you!"

When Danielle spoke she always had a way of touching David's heart; she always knew what, when, and how to say it. David never had someone in his life who spoke with such purity and truth, so when she spoke it would always touch him.

Danielle watched as he undressed in a sexual style that she always adored. He pulled his pants down, still a little emotional from a couple minutes ago. He folded his clothes up neatly and laid them on the side of the bed. Danielle noticed that David had lost a few pounds, but he was still cut like a bag of dope.

"Baby, go ahead and get comfortable. I'm uh hop in this tub real quick," David said.

"Oh, so you getting in the tub without me, that's how you feel?" Danielle grinned.

David didn't show the smile that he would normally, not being in a playful mood. Walking into the bathroom, he turned the water on, adjusting it to a lukewarm temperature. He grabbed the white rag and started covering it with soap, waiting for the water to fill up. When the water level reached midway, David used the tip of his toe to check and see if it was okay to sit in. Then he got in the tub and leaned back, closing his eyes and enjoying the soothing warm water. David desperately needed this time to relax and mellow out, and sat there in silence until his skin was soft and wrinkled.

"David, are you okay? You haven't made a sound in over twenty minutes."

"I'm cool, girl. Ya boy just enjoying this water, you feel me? I'm about to get up out of here in a few minutes."

"Okay," Danielle said.

David started rinsing his body off, and right before he was getting ready to sit back down, Danielle walked in. David was standing there covered with soap, off guard, not aware that his girl was going to come in.

"David, you acting real funny. It's like I'm not even here. You could have left me at home for all this."

"Girl, chill out. I told you I'm just going through some shit. I just needed some time to think, that's all," David said.

David didn't want Danielle getting any more upset then she already was. He knew all she wanted was to be held and get some dick.

David finished cleaning his body and pulled the plug to let the water down the drain. The water was filthy, leaving a slight ring of hair and dirt. David dried off while walking out of the bathroom. The anticipation of making love gave David a rush; he couldn't wait to make love to his pregnant girl.

"Come here, bookie. Come give daddy a kiss. I missed you."

"You don't miss me. You acting all funny," Danielle said.

David walked toward her, unraveling his towel from his waist. The towel fell onto the floor, dropping in front of Danielle's feet. The look, the glare in her eyes was like she hadn't been fucked in over a year.

"Come here, girl, tell daddy what you want. Tell me what position you want me to eat that pussy from."

David swung his dick side to side saying, "Girl, don't trip. They call me B.D.D., that's Big Dick Daddy."

It was things like this that kept the lumber lit in Danielle's fire place.

David had Danielle figured out. If her life was a book, he would have read every chapter. He knew what tickled her fantasy, what made her laugh, and what got her pussy wet. David was her first love, first kiss, and first one to enter her virgin love nest. Danielle started laughing as she enjoyed the entertainment; it never took long for her vagina to moisturize.

David laid down on the bed, looking Danielle up and down and realizing that she had gotten thicker. Everything grew: her breasts, her thighs, her calves, and her ass were bulging out of her dress. David enjoyed her thickness, using his fingertips to glide around her curvaceous body. He started massaging her scalp, running his fingers through her nice grade of hair. Danielle loved when David massaged her scalp, she actually started getting close to an orgasm whenever this was done to her.

Danielle wore a strawberry and cream thong with a matching bra set from Bloomingdales at the King Of Prussia mall in Philly. David loved seeing her in lingerie, which was a major turn on for him. He slid down her panties, drooling, melting, as he stared at her perfectly shaved vagina. David started kissing her with passion, holding her in his arms with the romance of a young prince. He laid her down on the bed, softly spreading her legs apart. The pressure was rising, intense, both of them breathing deeply in unison. Every kiss, every touch, shivered her body as if he cast a magical spell. The tiger in his eyes was enough to drive a porno girl insane.

"Oh, you were trying to keep that good pussy from me, huh. Damn, that's how you feel? All the good dick I done gave yo ass."

David loved talking shit and challenging Danielle to fuck him back. He started playing with her pussy, excited as her juices slid down her thighs. David placed one finger inside of her, going directly to her G spot. He had it mastered, perfected, and any time he gave this treatment to any girl they would explode. He started building up the rhythm; every few seconds he would tongue kiss her clitoris. He would swallow her, suck her, with a craving as if it was the last pussy he would ever taste.

"Oh, oh, damn. I love when you do that baby Please don't stop. Please," She used both of her hands pushing his head down.

Danielle would joke with David and call him, *Piranha Mouth Jaw Horn.* Danielle laid on the bed stretched out, as her body quivered from back to back orgasms. She was shaking, pulsing, her body locking up like Frankenstein. David was still fucking her without any scuba gear, enjoying every slip and every slide.

"Baby, I been thinking about this pussy every hour on the hour, I needed you badly. I want that ass in the air now, immediately, turn that ass over. So I guess it's true when they say pregnant pussy the best! Baby, if you could see this view, lawd."

David started massaging, caressing, and squeezing her ass with both of his hands. Danielle gathered her strength back and started making both of her ass cheeks bounce at the same time.

"Okay, okay, baby. I see you getting better and better. Let me find out you been practicing."

"I know what you like and what turns you on, so yes, I have been practicing. Watch this. I was watching one of the pornos you left in your bag and one of the guys made the girl bend over. She bent over and he put his dick on top of her ass. Then she started making his dick bounce side to side and I wanted to try it, it looked fun."

Danielle started bouncing her ass while David's dick bounced side to side on top of her lower back.

David was impressed. "Damn, boo, Daddy's proud of you, you a little monster now."

David spread open her butt cheeks admiring the beautiful vision that stood before him. No pimples, no stretch marks, the sight was beautiful, unscarred like the heavens. Danielle could never take David's large penis. He was hung like a horse and stiff as a rock. Everything about him spoke annihilator. So Danielle would make him start missionary until she was ready.

He was working the tip of his penis in a slow, smooth, and steady motion until her vagina walls would allow him to invade her body. She wrapped her arms around him, squeezing his body tighter every time he inched in further. David was trying to be careful, gentle; by all means, he didn't want to be tapping the top of his baby's head.

He was deep inside of her. She was warm, tight, and her moans softly echoed off the walls of the hotel room. David was sliding in and out of her easily because of her wetness. Danielle got on top of him and put her knees as far to his arm pits as possible. He pulled her closer to him and started French kissing her. Danielle was going at a light speed, enjoying the sensation, enjoying the thickness of the man she loved. She was going up and down, still fully moist; every time she would come down he would touch her spot. The shape of David's penis curved directly to her, so she would squirt every time she slid down onto him.

He couldn't hold it any longer, trying his hardest not to cum, but the feeling wasn't controllable. David's body tensed up as he approached orgasm, his body locked up and holding onto Danielle not being able to move. Danielle knew that he was getting ready to explode. She started speeding up, moaning louder, and screaming his name until he exploded. David needed it more than ever, and he was sexually relieved as he shot a thick wad of semen into her vagina. David told her how much he loved her, how much he missed her, and then they held each other until the next morning.

CHAPTER 6

THE SET UP

Trust no one

After a few days of making love, holding each other, and enjoying their time together, their stay was sadly finally up at the hotel room. Danielle, on the other hand, had to get back home before her mother went stir crazy. David was coming to grips that this could be the last time he would see his most prized possession. It was two places he was going: either Prison or a casket.

David helped Danielle pack her things, making sure she didn't leave anything behind, no I.D's, nothing that could trace back to her. He contemplated sending

Danielle home in a cab by herself. He thought about it for a few seconds having a hunch in his stomach that Danielle's mother was on some other shit.

Her mom wouldn't do that to me. She knows I'm the father of her grandchild.

David was going to enjoy his last ride with Danielle because he knew it was a chance that he would never see her again.

David locked all of his things inside of the security box except his jewelry and money. He figured he didn't need the jewelry for the journey that was upon him. He took the three diamond chains, the bracelet, and pinky ring and gave them to Danielle.

"Babe, all I have is sixty-five hundred dollars to my name. I'm-a have to give it to my lawyer; so I'm giving you five thousand of this. If this isn't enough for a lawyer then all of my jewelry is worth at least fifteen grand. You could sell it at a jewelry store in Philly on Market Street. They will give you at least twelve stacks for it. Just make sure you holler at the Italian guy that I always go to on Market Street. Baby, I need you more than ever. If this be the last time that I see you, tell my child that I loved him or her. Here goes my grandfather info he should be coming home in a couple months, and tell Pastor Tate thanks for the inspiration and for helping me find God."

"David, stop talking like this. You make it seem as if there is no chance." Danielle abruptly shifted into fear. "Why you think there's a chance you won't see me again?"

"That's not what I'm saying, baby. T, the Law, the streets of Harrisburg, want me out, they want me dead. These fuckin' pigs are trying to frame me. Listen, this is real shit, babe. I need you more than ever now. T, trust me, everything is going to be good. You're all that I have. Without you, my heart doesn't have a heartbeat. You're the blood that pumps through my veins, you're the only reason I want to live, you feel me?"

Danielle nodded, wrapping the money and jewelry up and placing everything inside of her bag. She picked up her phone and started dialing her mother's number.

"What are you doing? Who are you about to call?" David asked.

"I am calling my mom to make sure that she is home because I forgot my keys. Why what's the problem?"

"Oh okay. Nah, I was just asking because your mom was tripping before we left," David said.

Danielle knew that her mother wouldn't do anything to hurt her. She called her mother on the phone feeling bad, knowing the pain and stress that she had caused her.

"Mom, I am so sorry about the other day. I just needed to figure some things out that's all," Danielle said.

"Danielle, I was worried. I even called your father. He is very upset! Where are you, are you still with David?"

"Yes, mom, he is dropping me off in a few minutes, so please don't forget to leave the door unlocked because I forgot my keys," Danielle said.

"Okay, hurry up. We have much to talk about. I just finished cooking your favorite dish," Danielle's mother said.

David had been the type of person that always followed his instincts. He had a gut feeling that something wasn't right, but the trust of his angel blinded him.

They arrived at Danielle's house finally; the neighborhood was quiet as usual. Danielle lived closer to the suburbs, where the neighbors were older and there weren't too many kids around. David started to panic, getting more and more nervous. He started looking side to side, front and back, searching for anything that looked suspicious.

He got out of the cab, telling the cab driver, "I am staying in the cab, so leave the meter on and don't leave."

David opened the door for Danielle and walked her toward the steps of her house. He gave her a kiss and hug, telling her how much he loved her and that he needed her to stay in his corner. As David was walking away, he noticed her mother looking out of the blinds with a stone face.

Danielle made it inside of the house safely, and before she closed the door she turned around and said, "I love you, Baby. Call me as soon as you get back to the room."

David nodded with a face full of frustration. When he turned around, he wasn't surprised at all. The whole task force was everywhere, jumping out of the bushes, from behind cars, the neighbor's houses, to sharp shooters on the roof. They were all fully armed with large assault rifles, tear gas, and Teflon shields.

"Freeze, motherfucker. Let me see your fucking hands and don't move."

David went to raise his hands and they tazed him with the stun gun. He fell face first onto the concrete floor, shaking as volts of electricity ran through his body. They all had their weapons drawn with infrared beams pointed at his chest. He didn't have no choice but to surrender. He was surrounded. They had the whole area shut down. When David looked up at Danielle, she was snapping and trying to fight the police. She didn't respect nor agree as to how they were handling an unarmed man.

"That's not right. Y'all didn't have to stun, him he didn't resist arrest. Look at his fucking face. It isn't right, it isn't right! I want all of your badge numbers. Ooh, I hate the fucking cops," Danielle screamed.

Danielle's mother came outside and tried to pull her back inside of the house. "Girl, get your ass in this house. He is going where he belongs, jail. I called them, Danielle. I couldn't let you do this to yourself."

"Mom, I know you didn't call the cops, tell me you didn't do that? If you called the cops, I will never speak to you ever again."

Danielle stormed back outside of the door, seeing the cops with their knees in David's back putting the handcuffs on his wrists. They kicked him a few times, and then snatched him off of the ground, speed racing him to the paddy wagon.

"Yeah, we got your ass now. You see that pretty little girlfriend of yours? Get used to another man fucking her and raising that baby because you're never going to see that fine piece of ass again. It's going to be someone so deep in her you'll be forgotten in six months."

David walked with his head down, face bloody with one tear rolling down the side of his face. He looked up at Danielle, shaking his head as they shut the doors of the paddy wagon. David thought, *I should have gone with my gut feeling. I knew that bitch was going to do some hoe ass shit!*

CHAPTER 7

CAPTURED

All good a week ago

David sat in the police wagon pissed, his hands handcuffed tightly behind his back. He squirmed as he tried to get comfortable. It was hot, tight, with not much air to breathe. He stared, eyes watery, looking out of the two small windows covered in steel fence. He wasn't surprised that he was set up; he was more hurt than anything. He knew he should have went with his first instinct and never got inside of the cab with Danielle. In this game, rule number one is always go with your first instinct!

David was finally apprehended and on his way to York County Prison, from where he'd then be taken back to Harrisburg, Pennsylvania. When York County informed Dauphin County that they had David in custody, it took Dauphin County only two hours to come get him. Dauphin County police wanted David bad; they were pleased to know that he was now captured. It was only a twenty-five minute drive to York County, and the whole drive Danielle and the baby were the only things on poor David's mind.

The night was young; the sky full of energetic stars sparkling as if they were magical. The paddy wagon headed toward York County Prison. David could see the eyes of the animals that hid behind the trees and high grasses. He was thinking the whole time that the cops were going to pull over half way and kill him before they even got there. The whole way the cops were talking shit, getting angrier by the mile. When David felt the vehicle stop in a quiet area, he knew what was getting ready to go down. The doors opened up and both of the officers dragged David out of the van. They slammed him onto the ground and started beating him with their Billy clubs. They were two of the most racist, vile, sarcastic cops in York County. They took the hand cuffs off of David.

"Look, you fucking porch monkey, if you can kick both of our asses we will let you go. You'll be free as a bird." Both of the cops started laughing.

David knew even if he would seek victory, even if he was the victor they would never let him free. Both of the cops were big rednecks and one looked identical to the WWE wrestling star Brock Lesnar. The other looked like Arnold Schwarzenegger when he was back in his prime Commando/Predator days. David didn't stand a chance. All he could do was take the punishment. They jumped on him like two Tibetan Mastiffs jumping on a Chihuahua. After they got it out of their system, they put the cuffs back on his wrists and threw him back inside of the van.

"Well, boy, don't say we didn't give you a chance. You could have been free." The cops laughed.

David was laid out on the bench halfway dead, trying to catch his breath. The officers were smart, knowing not to punch him in the face, so they gave him all body shots. They got back in the Paddy wagon and pulled off. A few minutes later they were still driving up the back roads of York. Just as they got down the hill, out of nowhere a family of deer darted across the road. A big buck ran into the side of the paddy wagon, hitting it so hard that it nearly tipped over on its side.

"Oh shit, what the fuck? Aye, what the fuck is going on," David said with bare strength.

"We ran into a fucking deer. Shut your mouth and be quiet, niggar," the cop said.

"You stupid ass peckerwood, tobacco chewing motherfuckers. I'm ready for round two! You pale faced, little dick motherfuckers—that's why your wives want to fuck a black man." David tried his best to infuriate them. "You two trailer trash pussies won't dance with me one on one!"

The cops pulled over to the side of the road, tempted to bust David's ass open again. They needed to check the paddy wagon and make sure it was in good condition. They parked the van with their four-way signals on. The driver took his seat belt off and opened the door. He hopped out of the van telling the other officer to check on the captured.

"Go make sure that dickhead is okay. Put the rubber ball in his mouth. I don't want to hear that nigger's voice."

The driver walked to the side of the van with his flash light, and he didn't see anything but a dent on the side of the van. "Hey, Dan, the bastard didn't die. Lucky fucker—the deer got up and ran."

They both started laughing and hopped back inside of the paddy wagon. They put their seatbelts on and pulled off. When they arrived at York County Prison it looked like a mini college. For the moment,

David had no worries or concerns in York County—his issues were in Dauphin County Prison. He knew King was high power in Harrisburg and his army would be there waiting for him like a pack of starving wolves! David was thinking about his life and all of the blood that he had spilled. The men he violently took from their families and the souls of the innocent women he purposely tried to murder. Through all the pain, David knew that it was no time for weakness, fear, or mercy.

Two hours had passed. David couldn't fall asleep because his body was bruised from the cops that assaulted him earlier. Two correctional officers finally came and put their handcuffs around his wrists and walked him out to the transport van. The sheriffs were waiting for David to extradite him back to Dauphin County. He was already in a state of mind, already in preparation for what lay in front of him. Shit was about to get serious, crucial, and it was far from over. David was outnumbered, having no riders, no one having his back. He was too much of a soldier to ever go into protective custody! David would rather be remembered as a gangster than go out like a bitch with no honor, no glory, and no heart.

The sheriffs took David straight to Dauphin County Prison. As they drove past the Harrisburg East Mall, he showed a small smirk. He started reminiscing, having flash backs, of his glorious shopping days at Foot Locker, Styles WEST, and Macy's. He stared at the guards who walked with their K9 cop dogs. They had rifles strapped over their shoulder for a purpose. All of them were wearing dark black glasses patrolling their assigned area. They pulled inside of the county after the gate opened with a loud buzzer noise. The gate closed behind them as they parked the transport car. The sheriffs handed the extradition papers to the white shirt and walked him inside. They made David take a seat on the bench, so the sheriff could take the handcuffs off.

"It's cold as fuck in this bitch," David said.

The white shirts were cool. They weren't like the lower level C.O.'s. Their intentions weren't to hurt the inmates. They asked David what size he wore and handed him an orange jump suit with DOC in big white letters written across the back. David was all too familiar with those abbreviations: Department of Corrections. He was then handed a blue blanket and a plastic bag with a toothbrush and toothpaste inside. The sheriffs said their goodbyes to the C.O.'s and exited the facility. The C.O.'s took over from there and walked David to Q2, which was the classification block; the block that inmates go to when they first enter the jail. Inmates would stay on this block for three to five days until they were classified and ready to join population.

As David walked into the cell, he went straight to the window. The way the prison was set up, one could see the Harrisburg East Mall and Toys R Us right outside. David shook his head, staring at the filthy silver toilet, the rusted white sink. The corners of the cell were filled with garbage, roaches crawled up the wall, and the aroma of hot piss was present. He didn't know who was who, or who wanted him dead, so in his mind everybody was his adversary.

David stared deeply into the eyes of his celly, not flinching, not blinking, military minded and ready for whatever. His celly was a white man who kind of reminded him of Mr. Brown who molested him when he was younger. The white man was lying on the bottom bunk fast asleep. Once he noticed David, he immediately got up, grabbing his blanket and pillow to climb onto the top bunk. He wanted no problems, showing David the utmost respect by offering him the bottom bunk.

David wrapped his blanket around the thin blue mattress, making his bed to be laid in. He laid the rest of his things in the corner under his bunk. The condition of the jail didn't bother him at all. In his mind, he lived on the streets and came from nothing. David knew nothing would be more beautiful than yesterday from this day on. He resisted the urge to call Danielle in fear of her mother answering the phone. He knew she wouldn't give Danielle the phone anyway!

Three days later, David was now classified and on his way to C Block, which included prisoners who had a high bail, violent offenders, people who were facing big time. David and ten other inmates were chained together as two C.O.'s escorted them. They walked through the main hall of the jail where the blocks were located. This was how all the inmates got to see who was coming in the jail and who was going out of the jail. Dauphin County Prison stayed in an uproar, the inmates were all at their gates talking shit.

"You a dead man, David. Your face already on a T shirt boy," an inmate yelled, as he threw a cup of warm piss on him.

"Fuck you, bitch ass nigga. Remember, motherfucker, I'm not in here with ya'll, ya'll in here with me," he said, as he wiped the piss off of him.

David was now more angered than he'd ever been in his life. He hated for anyone to disrespect him. He figured that since he was a killer on the streets, the same rule applied in jail. He knew that it was going down once he hit C block, the most dangerous block in the prison. He walked into his new cell which was empty at the present. He looked around, seeing the room was much cleaner than his last cell. The first thing on his mind was finding something to make a weapon out of.

"I'm not boxing these old ass motherfuckers, this not the WWE. They getting stabbed from the rip."

So David grabbed his hard plastic toothbrush and started scraping it over top of a loose screw. He scraped and scraped until the tip of it was nice and sharp like a Native American spear. Next, he grabbed his pencil and wrapped the bottom of it in a thick layer of toilet paper. David looked in the mirror ready to embrace any altercation, thinking, *how can you kill what's already dead?*

When David's celly entered, he looked as if he had seen a ghost. He looked too familiar; David reached and grabbed his hawk in preparation to defend himself. David's memory came back: it was the young boy he sold the wet, coke, and pills to for that five hundred the one time. Even though David remembered him and did business with him, he still couldn't trust him.

"What's up, Bra? That was good looking on that work you sold me. I bubbled off of that, my nig!" David's celly said.

"Straight like that, lil bruh, as you should," David said keeping the conversation at a minimum.

David already had it in his mind that everyone was against him, thinking, *fuck friends, all I have are enemies*! It was him against the world, so the world, he was against. David was street smart, street savvy, and being a thinker he knew King would put a hit on his head. Dauphin County prison was cut throat, filled with people who would cut a guy's heart from his chest for ten dollars' worth of commissary. David had his guard up thinking, *fuck this shit, I'm not letting these hoe niggaz kill me.*

David's celly was persistent, and very diligent at trying to hold a conversation. David was in deep thought, getting angrier by the second, every word that his celly spoke angered him more and more. David balled up his fist, clenching his face and furling his eyebrows. He hopped up quickly, grabbing his weapon, and harshly poked it into the side of his celly's neck.

"Aye, nigga! Motherfuckers want me dead in this bitch. You want me dead, motherfucker?" David said with an angered voice.

"Bra, bra, bra, we from the same hood, Hill, the trill side, my boy. I don't fuck with none of these nut ass dudes!" David's celly said.

"Motherfucker, I have no hood. Fuck friends, I'm not shit, never have, never will be, nigga! Look, I'm at war, war ready. Stay the fuck out my way, bra!" David said, staring him in the eyes as he slowly took the hawk away from his neck.

David's celly stood there trembling, relieved, and knowing his life was in his hands. "Bra, I'm riding with you, my boy. Fuck them niggaz. I be warring with Lil L Trey from off the trinkle anyway. Them buster's just mobbed on me three months ago. I was hitting them pussy's with chairs and everything. I just got out of the hole last week, my boy! They all hustle for the boy King; that's why I am in here. I been posted on my block trapping all my life, they gone come and tell me that I have to cop from them in order to hustle on my block. They came through my hood on that bullshit. I let them fuck boys have it, lit they car up and hit Q-ball in the shoulder and Big Loc in the back."

The more his celly, Tom Cat, talked, the more David grew to not like him. He knew the elements of using victims as pawns; everything was a chess move to him.

CHAPTER 8

WAR READY

Dog is barely up

David's celly Tom Cat, had been incarcerated for a year and a half, waiting to go to trial for a hand gun, an ounce of crack, and attempted homicide. He knew all the beefs, he knew all the rumors, and knew who the targets were. He started breaking it down to David, telling him the gossip and who was on what blocks. David never told him why everyone wanted him dead, or who wanted him dead; his celly already knew. What goes on in the streets, the jail hears about it first. He told David all the blocks that King had goons on, and most of them were on C block. Most of them had gone home already after beating their cases. David knew that the fewer of them there was, the better. When Tom Cat informed him that Lil Sparky was on C block on the lower level, David knew it was going down. Lil Sparky was Smooth's hitter from the hill top in Harrisburg. Lil Sparky was a real nigga. He stayed on his goon shit full time, putting that work in. David had only been around him a few times, you know, handshakes, passing a couple blunts, nothing major. They were both young hot heads, both of them ready for war. David didn't trip for a second, already knowing he was much more of a savage! David was solid as a rock, a black rose, with nothing to live for; his heart and his soul were much colder.

After conversing with his celly it was now wreck time. You could either stay on the block or go to the gym. The gym was the spot everyone went to communicate, joke, or gossip about what happened on the streets. The gym was where all the blocks in the prison got the chance to interact with each other. They would separate the gym times like two blocks at a time, so it wasn't overcrowded. David knew this would be when he would see Sparky and everyone else he had done wrong. David was far from a pussy, far from ever being scared of any man living. He was going to approach his enemies, whether he be killed or they be killed. David walked out of his cell looking both ways with his weapon tucked. He walked down the stairs watching the other inmates, trying to familiarize himself with their faces. He was the youngest on the block, but he was feared and respected. At the end of the day, they knew he was a murderer.

As David walked inside of the gym, all eyes were on him. He was amongst the barracudas, anacondas, and all the older gangsters. He was all alone in jail with only his heart, balls, and his shank. David walked through the gym like he was 7 foot tall, 320 pounds. In his heart, he knew he had nothing to fear because he awaited death anyway.

Everyone still had their eyes on David, not blinking, and all with mean faces. The deeper David walked in the gym, the more faces grew familiar. He looked back at everyone with a look of no fear, with a look of death. David headed to the water fountain to get a quick sip, and he noticed four men were standing in the corner. It was Lil Sparky and two of the guys that were at the Waffle House a couple years back. David knew they were plotting, watching, waiting to see if he would panic.

David continued to sip his water, watching them out the corner of his eyes. After he had his drink, he stood on the wall with his shank in his hand. Lil Sparky and three other guys started walking toward him. They all walked with mean looking faces and gangster mannerisms. David started poking his chest out in position to defend himself, as the whole gym watched in anticipation, knowing something was about to go down!

"Yeah, we know you killed Smooth and shot our O.G King, it's too many cops and C.O.'s right now. On everything I love, bra, I'm a paint the jail red with your blood, bitch!" Sparky said

"What, bra? First of all, motherfucker, don't approach me with shit. I'm T.T.G: Trained to Go, my boy. Plus ya'll already know I get down, murder man slaughter. I got more bodies than you, dog!" David said as he showed his weapon.

"We will see, motherfucker," Sparky said and walked away, not wanting to draw too much attention.

No matter how hard or how strong, no man was tougher than the Dauphin County hole! People died in the hole from starvation, health complications, and suicide. Dauphin County was a modern day nut house. The chow they fed the inmates a motherfucker wouldn't feed to his dog!

Rec time was now over and the inmates had to go back to their cells. The C.O.'s escorted everyone from the gym, taking count as all of the inmates passed through the gate. David walked straight to his cell his face in a frown and his fists tightly clenched. He hated for anyone to approach him, especially on some gangster shit. He walked straight past his celly and laid down on his bed.

David started thinking about Danielle's mother setting him up and how he hadn't spoken to Danielle yet. David was concerned, wondering if she had taken the money to the Lawyer yet. He knew that any day she could receive her HIV test, and if it came back positive he knew things would get ugly. Danielle would for sure hate him, keep the money, take the baby, and never speak to or see him again. After an hour of thinking, David dosed off, lightly sleeping and waiting for dinner.

The C.O. that worked the second tier walked past and slipped a pink slip under the door, telling him that a lawyer was here to see him. David hopped out of the bed, picked up the slip, and started to read it. He was scheduled to see the doctor, so he could start receiving his medications. The door of his two-man cell had opened; David was happy and relieved that his lawyer was taken care of. David followed the C.O. down the tier, noticing Lil Sparky was a tier runner. They both caught eyes mean mugging each other as they walked past.

David arrived at the room where his lawyer was waiting; it was a White lawyer. The lawyer's name was Brian; he was a sure gun with a reputation for beating cases and making the best deals. The Lawyer had to be in his late thirties, his hair was short, brown, and his face cleanly shaven. Danielle obeyed David and paid the lawyer up front. Danielle hadn't received her results yet and still was waiting wondering why David hadn't called her.

"David," Brian Price said.

"Hey, wassup man. I hear that you're the man."

"I see that you have multiple charges. Let me see here. Well, you have two gun charges, a crack cocaine charge, and I see they're charging you for criminal transmission and/or attempted homicide. These are the only charges I see as of right now. I know that your girlfriend had mentioned something about them wanting you for murder."

"I ain't kill nobody, and what's this attempted homicide thing you're talking about?" David said.

"It says here that you were infecting women with HIV."

"That's crazy. I don't have the slightest idea what they're talking about," David replied.

Brian Price looked at David with a look of confidence. He was cocky, arrogant, and after looking over all the evidence he knew they didn't have enough evidence to convict him. "This is getting dropped at the preliminary."

When David got arrested, Danielle took Brian the money immediately. She gave him all of it up front, so he would make the case his priority. Brian did all of his homework—this was a high profile case. They knew David was involved in the shootout in York, but couldn't prove it. They knew he had relations with Portia when they found his ID in a pair of jeans at her apartment. They knew Cream was related to Smalls, and Smalls' gun was the same gun used to kill Cream, Portia, and Michael. With everything they knew, they still didn't have enough evidence to charge David with any of the murders. They had surveillance footage of a black female with Smooth in Atlantic City at the hotel. She was the last person seen with Smooth before he was murdered. The police scanned her face and it came back as Nu-Nu. When Brian told David that they had a female on the surveillance tapes, his belly instantly filled with butterflies. David knew she was the only thing that could bring him down. He didn't know what she would do once those people grabbed her; at the end of the day she's still a female. They hadn't found Nu-Nu for questioning yet; she would be in another town hiding once she got wind that the boys were on her top.

"Look here, man, I don't care what's true or false. All I know is that if there isn't any girl testifying that you gave her HIV, there's no case. David, if I were you, I would be checking into a civil lawsuit against the city. I mean, they're rambling rumors about your condition. That's slander. The other murders...I looked over that evidence and none of it is enough to charge you, so you're good. It doesn't matter if they think you did it or not, they have to prove it. So pretty much if this drug and gun charge wasn't here, you would be going home because your other gun charge we would just say it was Smooth's. It was his car and he is not alive to defend it, so you're good on that," Brian said

They didn't have nothing on him—all of his moves were strategically planned.

"That's what's up, bra. So what are they saying about the gun and drug charges?" David said.

"Don't worry about the drugs. I'm going to get it dropped down to personal use. Normally, since this is your first charge, I would get you probation, but since you're beating these other charges they're going to try to get you as much time as possible. The city of Harrisburg is not your best friend right now. So you will probably get a one to two, or a two to four at the most, so be happy. You'll be okay," Brian said.

Brian gathered all of his paperwork together, stacked them neatly, and put them back inside of his brief case. He got out of his chair and shook David's hand.

"Your girlfriend paid your fees up front, so stay out of trouble while you're in here. The murder charges were never filed. They wanted you for questioning, so if they decide to come question you, say nothing unless I am there. They have nothing, trust me. Take care, David, you'll be hearing from me soon."

CHAPTER 9

DETECTIVE

The hunt is on

fter meeting with his lawyer, David was relieved, convinced, and content that everything was going to be okay with his charges. He walked back to his cell smiling on the inside, but frowning on the outside. He had two soft spots in his heart and they were for Danielle and the baby only.

David made it back to his cell. His celly was working out doing push-ups, dips, and sit ups. David walked right passed him as if he heard the most horrifying news, playing it off and not wanting his celly to know his situation at all. "How that shit go, bra?" his celly said.

"They got your boy back against the wall. Shit real for a pimp, bra! They trying to keep a real nigga down. Fuck the world, fuck life, my only purpose is to die, bra!"

David sat down at the desk and started writing Danielle, expressing his feelings through writing. It was a chance that she would never get the letter there, but he had to at least try. He told her he was going to spend only a year in prison. He wrote the letter in blood and, with high hopes telling her this was a short journey, David finished the letter with a P.S., *"Always remember that you and the baby are all I have. Without you is like having a heart without a pulse*!!!!!"

He stamped the envelope and put the letter inside, using his tongue to stick it together. Then, he put the envelope under his mattress and laid down waiting for meal time. David's stomach couldn't bear Dauphin County's food. He was trying his hardest to forget about the hunger pains that intruded his empty belly. The jail's food was horrible, processed, and just enough to where you wouldn't starve. The night before commissary was the worst; with no money on his books, it was hard to enjoy watching the block feast in candies, cookies, and chips. The first thing that came to David's mind was running up inside of someone's cell and taking their commissary.

It was Rec time; David grabbed his blade and tucked it on the side of his waist. He had no intentions of going to the gym, figuring then would be the best time to run in someone's cell to confiscate their goodies.

"Hey, celly, which room is Lil Sparky's?"

"It's the fourth one on the second tier."

David was going to fuck Sparky up anyway, so he might as well take his shit. He waited for everyone to leave the block for gym, sitting in his cell waiting for the perfect moment. David was hungry; he'd never faced this type of starvation. He was becoming frail and nauseated; on top of that the retro-viral meds he was taking didn't make it any easier. David knew this would be a long process, at least three months. Three months in Dauphin County was like one year up state.

David walked down the tier, not caring if he was seen; he had his blade tucked just in case. David walked inside of the cell and took all of Sparky and his celly's commissary. He threw everything in one pillow case and walked out of their cell. He looked both ways, making sure the coast was clear. As he walked up the tier he saw that another inmate was watching him.

David looked at him and said, "What the fuck you looking at, bra?"

David continued walking up the tier, going into his cell. He was starving like a lost puppy searching through the trash for a bone. The first thing he did was empty the goodies onto his bed, with wide eyes trying to see what to eat first. In prison, going to another man's cell and taking his commissary is a death note. That's like going into a man's house and raping his wife, then killing his kids! David was relaxing, cooling, with a full belly waiting for the inmates to return from the gym. He was laughing inside, finding it comical what he'd just done. He couldn't wait to see Sparky's response.

"What the fuck, cuz. Oh y'all got me fucked up. I'm a kill a motherfucker! Somebody better tell me something or we gone punish everything moving on this block. Yo, Rocky, who the fuck went in my cell cuz?"

"It was the boy, David!"

"What the fuck? They took my shit, too. Oh hell nah, cuz!" Sparky's celly shouted.

Sparky had already known that David had something to do with it. He was the only one with nuts, with a heart to steal just like him.

"I know who did this shit, cuz."

"Who, nigga?"

"David, oh fiend ass. We gone fuck him up."

David was still sitting on his bed, amused, when he heard the commotion downstairs and started laughing out loud. He was making a smashy. A smashy is a jail house favorite that included: snickers, twix, and mixtures of other chocolates. Most of the inmates survived off of a smashy. The whole C block was in silence, not a sound from anyone. The only thing that could be heard was the rats running inside of the walls. Every few hours you could hear the C.O.'s walking through the tiers, doing cell check.

"Oh shit, my nig, you came up. Whose hut you hit my boy?" David's celly asked.

"You already know, man, that bitch ass Sparky. I had to get his hoe ass, you hear me?"

The next day had arrived and David knew that shit was about to get real. He was hoping a letter from Danielle would eventually arrive at his cell. It had been weeks and he still hadn't spoken to her. Whenever the Correctional Officer walked past and handed out mail, David would wait by the door. He had never gone a day without speaking to her since the first time he laid eyes on her. David laid in his bed wondering, staring at the ceiling. He wondered what she would do, or how would she react if she did have HIV?

Dauphin County prison was twenty-three and one out of the county. The majority of the time the jail was on lockdown. An hour had passed and a C.O. walked past David's cell.

"Get dressed. There's a couple detectives waiting to speak with you."

David figured nine times out of ten they were coming. His lawyer already informed him they would. David got dressed and walked to the room where the detectives were waiting for his arrival. One was black, stood at 6' 3" with a bald head, and a slim athletic build like he ran on the tread mill. The other was Hispanic.

"I finally get to speak with you. You're a highly wanted man on the streets of Harrisburg. Is there a reason why Calvin A.K.A. King has a price on your head?" the detective named Carter asked.

"Who, who the hell is King? I'm the only King I know, bra."

"Is that right? Then you wouldn't happen to know about the shootout in York a couple months ago? Sure you do because you were there, weren't you?"

Detective Carter reached in his briefcase and pulled out an envelope with a couple of pictures and showed them to David. David's heart started beating like a drum set on a drum line. It was pictures of Nu-Nu at the hotel on the surveillance.

"You wouldn't happen to know her, now would you?"

"Hey, bra, stop wasting my motherfucking time! You come all the way here for what reason? You already know I'm not talking. I have nothing to say. So keep it moving, my boy. If ya'll had something I would've been charged already. I'm done talking. If you have any more questions you can talk to my lawyer."

Carter started packing up his belongings and gave David a card. "If you have any questions, anything you would like to talk about, give me a call."

David stood there acting clueless, hands getting sweatier, trying to remain calm. When Detective Carter showed a picture of Nu-Nu, David thought, *Fuck, fuck, oh shit, they got Nu-Nu on surveillance.*

As Carter and the other detective were walking out of the room, Carter stated, "The cat got your tongue? You seem a little nervous. Why is that? I been around and seen killers for the last twenty years, some of the hardest cases, but I still found a way to bring them down. I know about the shootout in York. Portia and your I.D was in a pair of Levi jeans at her town house!"

"I never heard or seen a Portia in my life. This is a story that I'm not interested in trying to hear. So are you done, sir?" David asked.

"We have photos from the surveillance footage at the hotel of that fine little lady. As we are speaking now, we have Marshalls in Pittsburgh searching for Nu-Nu, and I'm quite sure she'll have some interesting information," Carter said

Carter and the other detective both started laughing.

David walked out of the room with a bubbly stomach; first thing that popped in his head was Nu-Nu. David went straight to his room to write Molt. He gave the letter to the inmate next door to send off for him. David wrote it in code, hoping Molt would read between the lines.

David now had another concern: if they were to find Nu-Nu, he was sure to go down. It would be a rap for him and he would spend the end of his days in Jail or even possibly get the needle.

"What's happening, celly? Don't let this shit stress you out, cuz. They can lock your body up but never your soul."

David had been ignoring Tom Cat for the past few days; he had been noticing a difference in his mannerisms. David couldn't trust himself, let alone trust another man.

Morning came and David finally decided to try and call Danielle again. After weeks of her mother denying his calls, eventually he gave up. David knew that she had to have gotten her test results back by now. Danielle never attempted to reach out to him, so he knew something was wrong.

CHAPTER 10

THE FIND OUT

When life changes

Danielle's life was in utter shambles and chaos; certainly not a way for a pregnant girl to live. Her father hated her, her mother crossed her, and she hadn't talked to David in weeks. Danielle was catching the city bus and cabs everywhere that she needed to go. She hadn't spoken to her mother since she set David up with the police sting. Danielle was in route to receive her test results. She walked off of the bus on her way into her doctor's office to her scheduled appointment. As soon as she walked inside she felt it in her stomach that the news she was receiving wasn't going to be good.

Danielle walked up to the front desk and signed in on the white sheet of paper. She gave them her insurance card, confirmed her information, and then sat down on the sofa to wait. The doctor's office was filled with pregnant women, some there with their baby's fathers and some alone. The doctor's office was comfortable with nice furniture, artwork on the walls, and a section with plenty of toys to keep the children occupied. There were portraits of happy families that lined the walls, and in every corner there was a flat screen television. Danielle sat there for twenty-five minutes patiently waiting for the doctor to call her name.

"Danielle," the nurse said.

"Yes."

"How are you feeling today?"

"I could be better," Danielle replied.

"Awww. You poor dear. Well follow me, I am going to need to take your blood pressure and check your weight," the nurse said.

The nurse took Danielle's weight, blood pressure, and escorted her to the room where she would be seen by the doctor. Danielle stayed silent the whole time, not smiling or conversing much. All that consumed her mind was what she would do, how she would live, and who would she tell if she was HIV positive. The nurse left the room and ten minutes later a doctor walked in smiling. This wasn't the doctor that she had seen before; this was a new doctor. Her normal doctor was an older white man in his late fifties with white hair and a pair of Steve Urkel glasses. She felt comfortable with him; Danielle became disturbed when seeing that her new doctor was younger, Asian, and in his late thirties. Danielle's face showed frustration, her palms were sweaty, and she couldn't keep her legs from shaking.

"Hello, my name is Dr. Tyrang, I am filling in as a Physician's Assistant for Dr. Williams. How are you feeling today? Any pains or discomfort with the pregnancy?"

"Listen, Doc, I have a funny feeling about this, so can you get straight to the point? Am I HIV positive?" Danielle asked

Doctor Tyrang sat down and took his prescription glasses off. He opened his folder and read the results sheet from bottom to top. He searched in his peripheral to find some sort of solace in Danielle's eyes. He couldn't bring himself to make eye contact with her. This was the part of his job that he never enjoyed.

"Doctor, just tell me, am I infected or what? I don't mean to be rude, but please just tell me and skip the small talk"

"I'm sorry to say this, but yes, you are HIV positive."

Danielle buried her face deep inside the palms of her hands. "My baby, will my baby have it, too?" Danielle asked.

"The baby will be just fine, and so will you as long as you take the medication properly. We have counselors and people who you can…"

Before he got a chance to finish his sentence, Danielle burst into tears. She grabbed her belongings and stormed out of the doctor's office. Danielle was in full shame, realizing she could never go on like this, she could never tell her parents that she was HIV positive.

Danielle left the office a dead woman walking. She was too ashamed to even get on the bus. She just wanted to walk; she already knew who had given her this incurable disease. Danielle felt every emotion one could feel at a time. She was filled with hate, rage, regret, and fear. The only thing she could think about was her father's words; the conversations he had with her about boys. Everything he tried to tell her now evaded her thoughts.

Danielle found herself sitting on the edge of a bench overlooking the Susquehanna River. *Why did God allow this to happen to me?* is all she kept thinking. She wanted desperately to fling herself into the water. Hoping that somehow the waves would cleanse her soul of the filth that lay within and, if not, then maybe God would be kind and allow her to drown, falling to the bottom, along with the rest of the scum of the Earth.

Strangely the wind didn't shift the same to her anymore. What once sounded like the swishing sounds of air passing, now sounded like whispers of souls from the darkness. Danielle watched in a stoic mode as two joggers ran past her. The people no longer looked alive. Time stood still, and Danielle knew that her life was now a ticking clock working in reverse.

CHAPTER 11

MAN DOWN

Bloody Rose

David figured by now that she had to have received her results. It was killing him softly not knowing if she was infected or not. David had sex with many women, purposely trying to give them HIV. He never thought twice about anyone's feelings, his only motto at the time was revenge on all women. When he met Danielle, he fell in love with her, longing for her to be happy with him. Now that he knew it was a ninety percent chance that he passed her his deadly curse, he could hardly stomach it.

"Father, I know I don't come to you often, but if you have any more remorse in your heart spare my evils. Let the only one I have in this life be safe. I will spare my life for hers."

David couldn't make a call until the next day, and he was growing more impatient and angered, prepared to take all of his frustrations out on anyone. He walked back to his cell, and as he was walking up the tier, he noticed Tom Cat passing signals to Lil Sparky. David kept moving, pretending he didn't see what he just saw. He felt a difference in his celly, his swing and his mannerisms were suddenly noticeable. David continued walking to his cell, being two steps ahead of them.

He grabbed a mop and snuck it inside of his cell; he knew that it was about to get ugly. He quickly started unscrewing the mop ring. He took the mop head and placed it next to the wall. In jail, when a signal is made, that means it's about to go down. Tom Cat had alerted Sparky that now was the perfect time. David poked his head out of his cell and saw Sparky coming one way and two other guys coming the other way. David picked up the mop stick, squeezing it, holding it tight as if he was playing baseball.

David thought, *I'm going to split one of these busters head's to the white meat.*

David laid his whack on the side of the toilet just in case as a backup weapon. He peeked out of his cell again and noticed there were two more men with them, making it six. He knew he was outnumbered; he had to think of something fast. David could see the shadow of his enemies, he felt the ground tremble, and he knew they were inches away from his cell. The first guy charged inside and David swung the mop stick, hitting him directly on top of his head. It made a loud *pop* as if a Lil 25 gun shot off. Blood started leaking down his face as his head split open like a watermelon. David quickly pushed him back out of the cell, shutting his door, laughing while they helped their wounded friend. Sparky tried to open the gate, but by then it was too late. The guards were already alerted and began making their way toward the altercation.

"It's on, nigga, my word on everything I love. When I catch you, bruh, I'm cut ya heart out, bitch," Sparky said.

"Whatever, pussy. He gone need a few stitches, some Tylenol, and some ice packs," David laughed.

David stayed in his cell cleaning up the blood from the inmate that just got his helmet cracked. He waited patiently for Tom Cat to return to the cell just so he could look him in the eye. He had a plan for him, to pay him back for betraying him. *I'm going to slit this fucker's throat ear to ear.* David always understood that the element of surprise was a motherfucker and the best way to strike your enemy. In jail, it was normal for somebody to get stabbed, swooped, or their heads busted.

Tom Cat walked into the cell as if nothing ever happened. He walked in quietly and poised, but not in his normal temperament. David knew he couldn't sleep another night with this snake in his cell. With no trust left, David was up all night like an owl planning his move for tomorrow morning.

It was 7 am, the time breakfast was served and it was now time for a shower. In county prison, showers were taken by tiers, starting from the top to the bottom. David grabbed his towel, rag, and his soap. He then started walking toward the shower prepared for anything. As he stepped into the shower room, he noticed only three people inside. David moved toward the shower head and turned the water on. His body odor was unpleasant, foul, and in desperate need of cleansing. He placed his head under the warm water, enjoying the sensations as the water ran down his entire body. David grabbed his soap and started covering his rag in it, cleansing his body thoroughly. He started reminiscing, thinking about the romantic showers he once enjoyed with Danielle. Rose petals, candles, R&B music, with a beautiful woman whose curvaceous body was covered in soap.

David was deep in thought, so deep that he wasn't on point, stupidly knowing his enemies awaited moments like this. As David started rinsing off his body, Lil Sparky and four other inmates stormed inside the shower area. David opened his eyes to his enemy, staring him dead in the face.

"Surprise, surprise! Look at this, cuz, this nigga slipping on banana peels. What, you thought shit was sweet? Nah, cuzzin, ain't no peace in my quarters. I told you I was at you ASAP," Sparky said.

David was outnumbered and without a weapon. He stood no chance. They had the shower blocked off, surrounding him like a pack of hungry wolves.

David grabbed his towel, drying himself. "Well it's gone be what it's gone be, motherfucker. I'm not scared to die, I'm already dead. Make your move."

David punched Sparky in the face, catching him square in the chin. Sparky fell flat on his ass sliding on the slippery floor, hitting his head. The bigger inmate out of all of them, grabbed David from behind, wrapping his massive arms around David in a bear hug. David tried to get away, but his strength wasn't where it would normally be due to his poor eating habits and decreasing health. The bigger inmate had David restrained, holding him so the rest of the crew could attack.

David tried to break the hold, and right as he tried to slip away, the bigger inmate body slammed David head first to the shower floor. Sparky got off of the ground and grabbed a sock he had tucked in his pants that was full of soap bars. He wrapped the sock around his wrist, tightly gripping it. He swung the sock back and then forward, hitting David on the side of his face.

SMACK.

David's eyes rolled into the back of his head, his arms locked in the air like Frankenstein's monster. Blood started leaking down the side of his face as he laid stretched out on the ground shaking. When David hit the floor, they showed no remorse to the fact that he was already knocked out cold. They all started stomping and kicking him in his face, his stomach, rib cage, and anywhere else they could cause damage.

"Aye, fuck this shit, cuz. He killed the big homie Smooth. Tiny Toe, rape this fuck boy and leave his ass wide open; hurry up!" Sparky said.

Tiny Toe was light skinned with tattoos all over his body from head to toe. He was 6' 4", two-hundred and seventy pounds and represented the thirteenth street projects. He was a soldier, a killer, and most of all he was gay. They called him Tiny Toe because he was gigantic with tiny toes. Besides him being gay, he was a down ass nigga with zero tolerance. King used him for sending messages and those messages usually set an example. His motto was leave their enemies naked with split asses.

Tiny Toe laid David on his stomach, spreading his legs apart, getting ready to enjoy himself. David was still knocked out and was losing blood fast. Tiny Toe laid on top of David while Sparky and the rest of the gang left the shower.

"I got this, cuz. Don't worry, I'm a split is ass apart good!" Tiny Toe said.

Tiny Toe positioned himself on top of David full throttle with his dick in his hand. Right before he was about to penetrate, a guard walked in.

"Hey, what the fuck are you doing, guards, guards!" the C.O. yelled.

He blew his whistle for help and all of the guards rushed toward the showers. They started beating Tiny Toe with wooden sticks, speed balling him to the hole.

"Inmate down, inmate down. Level six, he's hurt badly. Code Red...Code Red! Call medical down here now!" the guard yelled.

The guards were not able to get him to his feet; he was knocked out cold. If they wouldn't have arrived when they did, he would have been raped, too. They rushed him to the hospital, so he could get proper medical treatment.

David was in a comatose state.

CHAPTER 12

ANGRY FATHER

Daddy's little Girl

D anielle was losing weight fast, thighs less thick than they used to be, and her ass decreased two sizes. With everything going wrong in her life, she couldn't handle the pressures of living with HIV. Every day that passed by the thoughts of David, the baby, and the relationship between her and her mother seemed beyond fixable. Danielle's father was on his way back from East Berlin, Germany. He always traveled, making long business flights, so it was nothing to him. A couple of drinks, some snacks, and he was good to go.

After a twelve hour flight, Devon got off the plane and headed toward the main entrance. He'd expected his angel to be waiting for him with open arms, but surprisingly he didn't see anyone. He called Danielle's mother to see where they were so they could pick him up.

"Hey, I just got off the plane. I'm headed to get my luggage. Are ya'll here yet?"

"Yes, I'm out front," Danielle's mother replied.

"Okay, see you in a few minutes."

Danielle's father was standing, waiting patiently by the luggage claim for his bags. He looked at his sports watch to see what time it was, then reached in his pocket and pulled out his cell phone to dial his girlfriend's number.

"Hey, sweetie, I made it here safely. Tell Karajan that Daddy love's her and I'll be home in a couple days."

He grabbed his luggage and started walking toward the exit door. He walked with a Marine's posture, his face shaved clean and his head bald and shiny like Mr. Clean. He opened up the door and walked outside, looking both ways, not realizing Danielle's mother was parked in front of him. He smiled, happy to see his ex. They didn't see eye to eye about the Marine life—Danielle's mother grew weary of the constant moving and making new friends. Other than that, they shared wonderful eighteen years together. He would always love her.

He peered inside the car, trying to find Danielle, but noticed she wasn't there.

"Where is my daughter?" he asked.

"I don't know. She doesn't communicate or talk to me anymore. I don't know where she is," Danielle's mother replied.

"What the hell you mean, you don't know where she is?"

His attitude, posture, and tone changed dramatically as steam released from his pores. Danielle's mother had previously informed him about Danielle's pregnancy and how she was pregnant by a boy wanted for murder. The last time he saw his princess she was still a virgin, innocent to the cruelties of life. When Danielle's mother became bored and tired of her husband flying country to country, she no longer wanted, nor desired, to be in a relationship and gave him an ultimatum. Danielle's father was a diehard Marine man—his dream, passion, and goal to retire as Commander in Chief would prove precedent over his family, costing him everything.

Danielle's mother returned home some few hours later with her father; the neighborhood still quiet and motionless. Devon hated Pennsylvania, only coming to town to see what was going on with his daughter. He planned to stay for two or three days and then he would have to go to Washington D.C. for another assignment.

"So what's going on with my daughter? Where is she?" Devon asked.

"She's not speaking to me," Danielle's mother said. "She knows my work schedule, so she makes sure we're not here at the same time. I don't know what else to do, I think I've lost her."

"So she's pregnant, how did this happen? Matter fact, don't answer that...I left my baby girl a rising star and now she's pregnant."

"Look, I work all day. And I do have a life, also. I can't baby-sit her Twenty-four seven, not to mention I can't even control her—she doesn't listen to me."

"I understand that, but are you hearing yourself, Christine? You said my baby was pregnant by a murderer, a guy who is supposed to have HIV?" her father questioned.

"Well, that's what the news said. He's in jail right now. I asked Danielle what was going on, but she won't tell me anything. She hates me!" Christine replied tearfully.

"What's her number? I'm going to call her and find out what's going on for myself."

Danielle's father tried calling her, but she wouldn't answer. He left four voice messages letting her know that he was in town for a few days. He called and called until she finally answered.

"Danielle, this is your father. Where are you, sweetheart? I'm at   your mother's house."

"Hey, dad, I didn't know you were coming to town I'm over at my friend's house, but I'm not coming over there."

"Okay, where are you? I'm going to come and get you," her father replied.

Danielle told him her location and he left immediately to go and see what was going on with his daughter. Approximately fifteen minutes later he pulled up in Christine's car to the address Danielle had given him. He honked the horn and within two minutes Danielle walked outside. She was happy to see her father, but at the same time still felt out of place. Danielle felt as if they'd all swam out to the middle of the ocean as one happy family, for him to swim away and watch them drown, leaving her broken hearted.

Danielle held all of these feelings and emotions inside, which made her easily susceptible to David's manly presence. She knew what her father wanted to talk about. He would always remain calm until he got around you, and then he would flip out. Danielle walked down the steps, holding the rail for support. Her father got out of the car to help her inside the vehicle, shutting the door for her.

"So how have you been?" he asked.

"I've been better. As you can see, I have a baby on the way," Danielle stated.

"I see, so why do I have to be the last one to find out? Why haven't you called me, Danielle? I am still your father."

She remained silent, not saying anything knowing where the conversation was heading.

"Your mother said she hasn't spoken to you in weeks. What's going on? This is not you, Danielle. I don't recognize this person you've become, you're better than this. Who is this David guy your mother keeps talking about? She's saying that he's a murderer and supposedly has AIDS?"

Danielle couldn't find it in herself to speak, still sitting there trembling, scared to respond. Her father was becoming angry and frustrated; he hated to be ignored or disobeyed.

"Danielle, I didn't fly seven hours over the ocean for you to just   ignore me. I am your father. Tell me what the *hell* is going on? You were not raised this way. I didn't raise you to go and sleep around with killers and get pregnant!"

Danielle's father was in full rage now, shouting his words while swerving down the street.

"*Dad, watch out,*" Danielle yelled!

Danielle's father swerved back into the correct lane, gaining his composure. He stopped and pulled over, knowing things were ready to get out of hand. "Danielle, I don't know what has gotten into you."

Danielle used the sleeve of her shirt and wiped the tears and snot from her face off. "You want to know, *right*. Well, you would've known if you didn't desert me. You chose the military, your job, over me and mom, so this is your fault. I hate you, I hate mom, and I wish that I was never born!" Danielle screamed.

As she opened the door, tears fell from her eyes. She didn't have the willpower to tell her father she was HIV positive.

"Don't worry about me, like it's always been. Be happy living your life in Germany. I hope you find comfort knowing you saved the whole entire world, but couldn't even save your own daughter. I don't need you, mommy, or anybody!" Danielle hopped out of the car, leaving the door open.

"*Danielle! Danielle!*" her father screamed.

She never looked back, and continued walking back to her friend's house.

Devon drove away confused, shattered; the truth of his daughter's words cut through him like a samurai sword. He knew he'd lost his daughter. Not knowing what to do, he packed up and left for D.C. the next morning.

Danielle continued walking until she was too overwhelmed to go on. She crossed over Third Street to a Subway restaurant, where she went inside to use the restroom. Danielle looked in the mirror and grabbed a paper towel to wipe off her face and blow her nose. She was devastated; for the first time in her life she felt alone. She sat on the toilet and cried for what seemed like hours, asking God for guidance. She had no one to call, no shoulder to lean on, and she didn't want to tell anyone that she was infected. Danielle thought about David, the baby, her father, and how she had let everyone down. She couldn't take it anymore. She wasn't like David; her heart wasn't cold as the artic sea. The thought of dying, rotting away, was eating away at her. Every day that passed she lost more and more hope.

CHAPTER 13

HOLD YA HEAD

What would you do

Danielle was tired of dealing with the shame, tired of going through it with her mother and father. She felt bad for breaking her father's heart. She kept her secret locked in a bottomless den, which only made the situation worse. Her mother tried reaching out to their family Pastor for guidance. Pastor Tate was like a father to Danielle. He tried calling her several times, not wanting to give up on her; he, too, didn't understand the sudden disappearance from service or her lack of communication. Danielle's mother told Pastor Tate everything, unable to keep truths from him. He was their spiritual mentor.

Pastor Tate wanted desperately to talk to Danielle, so he acted as if he didn't know what was going on. He left a text message for her to come to church on Sunday and have dinner somewhere after the service. Their relationship was bonded by God and love. If Danielle had nothing else in life, she had him. She went from being a church girl from Atlanta, Georgia to a pregnant HIV positive patient. She couldn't understand why the lord would allow a person like David into her life. She lived by his word and, for this to happen, she couldn't understand.

Danielle finally made it back to her friend's house. She knocked on the door and waited for her friend to let her in. Danielle knew she was overstaying her welcome. Everyone around her seemed easily agitated by her presence, and she could feel the vibe throughout the house. She wasn't eating, wasn't coming out of the room as much, and pretty much stayed out of everyone's way. There were three people who resided in her friend, Stacy's, home and, every so often, a different man came to visit her friend's mother.

Stacy had a job interview in the morning, and, normally, Danielle would have gone with her, but she wasn't feeling too good. She had an upset stomach and wanted to stay in bed. Stacy's mother had gone to work late, over sleeping from having a long night with her company. Danielle could hear the bed squeaking, loud moans, and conversation all night. Stacy's mother enjoyed a man's company, making her own music every other night.

Shawn, Stacy's mother's friend, decided to stay at the house and wait for her to get off work. Danielle had no idea she was left alone with a grown man in the house, so she figured it was cool when she decided to go into the kitchen with just her t-shirt and panties on; a lime green panty set from Victoria Secret that David had bought her.

She opened the refrigerator door and grabbed the milk carton, then looked through the cabinets, trying to choose between Captain Crunch and Fruity Pebbles. As she was pouring the cereal into a bowl, she heard footsteps coming down the stairs.

Oh shit! Who the fuck is that? She waited a couple seconds to see who it was and, to her surprise, it was her friend's mother's date. He walked into the kitchen with his shirt off, a tattoo of a dragon on his left shoulder catching her eye. He had a reputation in the city as being a dog and a pervert. It was also known that he enjoyed tricking off with underage women.

"Goddamn! How old are you? You look good as fuck!" Shawn said.

Danielle couldn't believe it. She left her unfinished bowl of cereal on the countertop and tried to barge past him. Shawn stopped her by getting a firm hold of her butt cheek. He cupped her bottom with the palm of his hand, trying to feel her vagina through her panties.

Danielle tried to get away, slapping him across his face. "What are you doing? Get your hands off of me!"

Shawn got upset and pushed her in the back of her head with light strength. Danielle tripped forward, barely catching her balance. She ran up the stairs crying, feeling violated, and locked the door behind her. Danielle got dressed quickly; she put on some sweat pants and Nike tennis shoes. She snatched up her pepper spray thinking, *I'm getting the fuck out of here.* Danielle didn't know if she should leave it alone or tell her friend's mom what happened. Not wanting to cause more tension in the house, Danielle decided keeping it to herself was the best way to handle things, thinking *they already acting funny toward me.*

Stacy felt as if Danielle needed to go home and talk things out with her mother.

"Danielle, you know I love you. You're my best friend in the whole wide world. Sis, I care about you and the baby. I think you should go and talk to your mother," she stated gently.

Danielle wasn't trying to hear that at all, instead taking her statements as a hint that she no longer wanted her around. After the situation with Shawn, she was petrified and didn't want to rest her head another night there. She was emotional—everything made her upset. She felt like everyone was out to get her.

"You could've said that you wanted me to get out. I felt the vibe a while ago. I'm going to stay at a shelter, away from the world, so that way I won't be a burden to anyone," Danielle responded.

Danielle started packing her belongings, throwing everything inside of her duffle bag in a hurry. As she was frantically packing all of her things, her bottle of retrovirus meds fell to the floor. Danielle quickly reached down to pick up the bottle of pills, but her friend was closer and grabbed them up before she had a chance to retrieve them. Stacy took a glance over the bottle, the prescription was for Atripla, a known medical treatment for HIV. When Danielle stood up she realized that Stacy was reading her medicine bottle. Danielle lost her sanity and cool, forgetting her knowledge of the lord. Danielle snapped, highly upset that her friend may know of her status.

She snatched the pills back from her friend. "Get the fuck away from me."

"Sis tell me them aren't the pills I think they are. I just seen a commercial with that same bottle. Oh my god, Danielle, talk to me! If those are what I think they are, you need to talk to someone. You can't keep all this bottled up inside of yourself. You will only destroy yourself faster."

Danielle didn't know what to think, all she knew was that she didn't want anyone to know her situation. Her eyes filled with tears as she walked straight past her best friend, ignoring her.

Stacy stood there bewildered. All she could do was shed a tear knowing the pills were exactly what she thought they were.

Danielle stormed out of the house. She now had nowhere to go, leaving her no other choice but to go home. Her mind raced a hundred miles a minute. Stacy was known to have a big mouth, and it was only a matter of time before her secret was out. She was weak, barely able to carry her belongings. Danielle's life had hit rock bottom, and she couldn't take it anymore, she needed her mother. Danielle stopped at a corner store to take a breather, exhausted from all the stress and the pregnancy. She pulled out her cell phone and dialed her mother's number.

"Mom," she said in whisper.

"Danielle, baby, where are—are you okay?" her mother asked in a panic.

"I'm at the A plus across the street from the Spanish restaurant. I'm ready to come back home," Danielle cried

"I will be there in less than five minutes. I'm coming to get you."

When Christine heard her daughter's voice in tears, her motherly spirit came into play instantly. She hadn't talked to her in a while, and she was worried, concerned and praying she didn't lose her forever. She pulled up alongside the gas pump at the A Plus, her tank on empty. She pushed the button to open the gas cap and opened the door. She scanned the parking area for Danielle, and spotted her standing inside of the A plus. Christine hurriedly got out of her car to help Danielle with her bags. She shut the trunk, then walked toward her pregnant sixteen year old daughter to comfort her.

Danielle stood there with a face full of sadness with bags beneath her puppy eyes. Without any hesitation, she walked into her mother's arms and wept until her feet felt weightless beneath her. After months of thinking, Danielle came to grips that her mother was the only person she had now.

"Mom, I am so sorry, please forgive me," Danielle said.

"Baby, we can talk about this another time, right now I'm just happy your safe and in one piece," her mother said.

They got inside of the vehicle, put their seat belts on, and pulled off. It was a silent ride to the house, so much emotion and so much pain clouded the air. They pulled up to the house and parked the car. Danielle's mother got out first and opened the door for Danielle, telling her to go inside and get some rest and she would be in shortly. Danielle was still in sorrow, still down in spirit, and her mother could see it clearly in her face. Her mother understood she was going through something, she knew that something was different and bothering her.

Danielle was taking the medicine regularly but wasn't eating as much because the medicine would upset her stomach. She knew that she had to eat in order for her and the baby to survive. It had been a minute since she heard anything from David. Danielle had no idea that he was in a coma, she assumed that he gave her AIDs and abandoned her. Danielle was stressed out and couldn't take it anymore thoughts of suicide infiltrated her mind on a daily basis. She didn't want to die but at the same time she didn't want to live. Danielle laid across her bed still heavily burdened leaving the sheets wet from the tears that she shed. Her harmless innocent mind wasn't prepared for this war. She couldn't believe the first time she made love; she would enlist to be punished with an incurable disease forever.

CHAPTER 14

SAD SONG

Prayers in an envelope

Danielle stayed in bed the entire day, with a box of napkins to dry her tears. Her cries echoed throughout the house, bouncing off the walls that once filled her happy home.

"Danielle, baby, are you okay? Come down stairs so we can talk. I'm here for you; we can talk about anything." She paused after hearing no response. "Look, I know I shouldn't have called the cops on David, but I was scared and didn't know what else to do. I can't take back what I did, but I'm still your mother and I will always love you no matter what."

1

Danielle was tired of holding everything in; it was killing her, draining her spirit. She finally gathered the courage and strength to let her mother know her condition. "I love you so much, and it breaks my heart to know that I broke yours. There is no other way to tell you, so I am just going to say it. Mom, I have HIV and I am going to die. I am going to die, mom!" Danielle cried.

The look on Christine's face was like she'd just seen a ghost. She started rubbing her forehead, the anger and emotion building up. Her face turned beet red and sweat began releasing from her pores. She didn't know what to say or how to respond. She was beyond pissed at her daughter and the decisions she'd made.

"No, no, Danielle, what have you done? How could you allow this to happen? I raised you better than this. You were a straight "A" student. No, no, please tell me this is not true. I told your ass, I specifically told you to follow the path of the Lord. You know once you stray from the righteous path you open yourself up to all the evil in the world. That boy is the devil. The first time I looked into his eye's, I could feel my soul burn. Now look at you? You ruined your life for a cheap thrill, and now have to live the rest of your days out like an infested whore! I'm so disappointed in you, ashamed of you, and want nothing else to do with you! God doesn't like ugly and has his way of seeking revenge."

Danielle's mother crushed her deeper and deeper with every word. Danielle ran up the stairs to her bedroom devastated, more heartbroken than before. She started searching through her drawers for a pen and a piece of paper. She found what she was looking for and started writing.

I'm sorry that I let you and dad down, but I can't and I won't live as a HIV patient. I can't take it, I'm not strong enough to live this way. What you said was true mom and for that reason I don't deserve to live. Why me? I gave my life to the Lord, I was at church every Sunday. He was supposed to protect me I believed in his word. So please don't mourn me I'm happier this way. Me and the baby are going to hell and will live out eternity there. This is what GOD wanted he didn't accept me mom. You said the lord would always love me that he would always watch over me as a father does. So why wasn't I worthy of heaven? He allowed this spawn, child of Satan to enter my life, and infect me! Please tell David that I and the baby love him and will be waiting at the Devil's playground for him to arrive! Tell Pastor Tate that he was like a father to me and I love him.

Danielle left the note on her dresser and stormed out of the house frustrated, weak, and exhausted from her pregnancy. Her mother wanted to apologize, trying to stop her, but it was nothing she could do. Her words had scorned Danielle to the soul. Danielle didn't really have a destination in mind, but what she did know was today would be the last for her and her unborn child. She remembered one of her favorite places she'd visit, where she could see the entire city view. When Danielle first moved to PA, she'd go to this spot on top of this apartment building to find solace and peace. It was an older building with eighteen floors and one elevator. From the top of the building one could see the whole city, it was beautiful; the tall buildings downtown, the sun rising and falling over the landscape. A perfect scenery to a gruesome end.

Danielle got onto the elevator, pushing the eighteenth floor button. It felt like twenty hours had passed before she arrived at the top. Danielle's body was trembling and shaking, a million thoughts racing through her brain. She was a child of God and always abided by his rules, for the most part. When she became infected with HIV, she lost all sight and hope, her soul gone and she not strong enough to live without it.

She finally made it to the top of the building and got off of the elevator, heading toward the roof top exit. She knew in her heart that she was wrong and was in total violation of God's rules. She was not only thinking of taking her life, but the baby's life as well. She assumed the baby was going to catch this dreadful virus, not believing the doctor's at all.

The sky was beautiful; the clouds bright white, full, and thick as if the heavens awaited her. The clouds looked like faces, faces of fallen soldiers that were accepted through the pearly gates. You could see the smoke lines from the jets that zoomed past. Danielle loved and cherished every sight, every smell, and every sound. She walked closer to the edge, staring into the sky, crying while holding her bulging belly. Walking to the edge of the roof, the wind traveled through her hair sending a wave over her body as gravity pulled her closer to the rim. Pebbles fell from under her feet as she inched herself closer and closer to the ledge. Danielle had already made up her mind that it was too late for anyone to save her now. Right before she was getting ready to jump off the roof, a man from across the street yelled.

"Hey! Hey, what are you doing? Hey! Hey!" he yelled at the top of his lungs.

Danielle looked down, quickly gaining her senses and realizing how small the people and cars were from up there. She hated heights. Taking a deep breathe, she backed away from the ledge. She slid down the side of the brick wall connected to the roof, catching her breath as she realized how close she'd come to knocking on death's door.

Danielle left from the building still frustrated and not in her right mind. Still determined to kill herself, she just didn't have the guts to jump off the roof.

Danielle walked back home, arriving to an empty house. She traveled through the house, turning on the lights, happy she was home alone. Every time she passed by a mirror, it reminded her that she was a dead girl walking.

She knew her mother would be home shortly, and she more than likely hadn't read the suicide letter yet. Danielle went to her bedroom and, upon opening the door, the first thing she noticed was the big pink teddy bear David had won for her at the carnival last summer. She grabbed two sheets and tied both of them together tightly. Then she tied them around her bed post because it was the sturdiest thing in her room. She was tired of living. It wasn't the fact that she had HIV, it was the shame and disappointment that she couldn't live with. It was around 4:30 in the evening and the sun was still beaming rays through the blue sky.

Danielle's mother got off of work at 4:00, so she knew that at any minute she would be walking in. Danielle went to her knee's praying out loud, making sure that God heard her loud and clear. After she spoke to her lord, she was ready to proceed in her mission. Danielle tied a knot just big enough for her head to fit in, and made sure that it was tight. Not being able to stop shaking made it hard for her to put the sheets around her neck properly. She opened up the window, making sure there wasn't anyone watching.

As she was sticking her leg out of the window, she heard her mother opening the front door and placing her purse on the counter-top. She then took her work bag off of her shoulder and placed it inside the closet. She looked around, realizing that Danielle wasn't downstairs like she normally would be, so she headed upstairs. After their horrible fight earlier she wanted to show Danielle that she truly was in her corner. She knew that she'd crushed her daughter's heart into shattered pieces; it had been tearing her up on the inside hourly. She wanted to tell her that she still could live a normal happy life as long as they stuck together as a family. She continued up the stairs, wondering why it was so quiet.

Danielle heard her mother walking up the steps, knowing she was coming to her room to check on her. Scared and heart racing, she didn't have the will to continue living her life as an HIV victim.

As bad as she wanted to live her life and not commit suicide, she figured it was already a part of God's plan. She stuck her right leg out of the window, inching half of her body out. Losing her balance, she slipped out of the window. She hung by the neck, choking, gasping for her last breath. Her legs kicked as she tried with her hands to remove the bed sheet from around her throat. The pain was massive, which made her want to live at the moment of her bad decision. With all of her might she slightly got her hand between the sheets, giving her a few extra seconds. Danielle thought she wanted to die, but she wasn't ready to kill herself.

As she was dying, every memory passed through her head: David, her mother, her father, the baby and she realized she wanted to live now.

Danielle's mother knew something wasn't right. She made it to the door and opened it, looking side to side, but not seeing her pregnant daughter. As she looked around, she realized that the window was open and a sheet tied to the bed led out of the window. She frantically ran to the window seeing her daughter hanging from the bed sheet. Danielle looked up at her mother with tears overfilling her innocent eyes. Her mother was screaming at the top of her lungs, trying to pull her heavy body up, but it was too late. Danielle stopped kicking, stopped choking, stopped moving; she was lifeless in front of her mother on eyes.

"No! Help, please, somebody help me. Not my baby, not my baby!" her mother screamed. With all of her strength, might, and willpower she started pulling Danielle up; close enough to pull her up through the window. She was hysteric, unraveling the sheet from around her daughter's neck. Danielle's face was swollen, black and blue, her tongue hanging out of her mouth and her eyes rolled up to the back of her head.

While all this was going on, an old black lady across the street had seen Danielle hanging from the window and had already called the ambulance and police. The ambulance was close since the hospital was right around the corner. They pulled up two minutes later to come to the rescue, but it was too late. She was already dead. Danielle committed suicide at the age of sixteen.

Danielle's mother cried and cried; she couldn't believe what her daughter had done. She was devastated, knowing her words encouraged her daughter to do the unthinkable. It was the worst day of her life losing her daughter to suicide and, on top of that, the thought of the baby dying was unbearable. Danielle's mother hopped in the ambulance as they tried to save the baby. All she could do now was pray and leave it up to God! They only had five to ten minutes to get the baby out of her belly before the baby died from lack of oxygen.

"How long has the mother been dead?" the ambulance lady asked.

"Only a couple minutes," Christine replied. "When I got here she was already dying. She looked at me before she died, reaching for me to help her. I was too late—I should have been there for her!" Danielle's mother wept uncontrollably.

"Come on, guys, we only have a few minutes to save this baby," the ambulance driver yelled. "Speed it up!"

Danielle's mother sat there devastated and in shock; it was too much to handle watching them trying to save her grandchild. They arrived at the hospital within five minutes and parked in front of the emergency room. The ambulance drivers opened up the door and pulled out the stretcher with Danielle and her unborn baby on top of it. Danielle was pronounced dead on the scene. They still had to put IV's in her arms and an oxygen mask, so the baby could breathe. When Danielle's heart stopped beating, the baby began to suffocate, losing oxygen to its brain.

Danielle's mother waited in the family room for the doctors to come back with word on her condition. She sat there in the corner crying, shaking, and not knowing what to do. She tried to call Danielle's father, but the call went straight to voicemail, plus the cellular signal was horrible inside of the hospital. The emergency room was overcrowded; they all felt sorry as Christine poured her heart out.

Then, Danielle's mother heard a familiar voice coming from the crowd, getting closer by the second. She looked up and wiped the tears from her face. It was Pastor Tate and his wife. They both ran over and hugged her, holding her in their welcoming arms. All in utter shock, they wondered how God could allow something like this to happen.

When Pastor Tate received wind of what happened, he and his wife immediately came down to the hospital. Danielle was like a daughter to Pastor Tate, so when he heard that she killed herself he broke down into tears. They all cried together, praying that lord showed mercy and let the baby live. A nurse came into the family room, asking the immediate family to follow her. She escorted them to a private room and told them a doctor would be in shortly.

Minutes later, the door opened and two doctors came in. "She made it. We got her out just in time."

The doctors were happy to report good news that the baby girl had survived, but were saddened at the same time. They saw the sorrow that filled the family's desperate eyes. The emergency room was packed with patients suffering from stab wounds to gunshot wounds; it was a crazy day in York, Pennsylvania. The news reporters were present conducting live interviews.

All the local news stations talked about Danielle and the baby for three days straight, stating how they couldn't understand how this promising young honor student, who respected God so much, could have brought her life to such a tragic end.

CHAPTER 15

NEVER DIE

A soldier dies once

Three months had passed and David still hadn't awakened from his coma. He laid in the hospital bed with IV's in his arms as still as the dead. The doctors had stitched David's head back together, bandaged his body in a cast so his ribs could heal, and the swelling in his face was back to normal. Every few hours a nurse came and checked on him to make sure he was okay. They were expecting him to come out of his coma any day now. The doctors noticed David's fingers and eyelids beginning to twitch more and more.

It was 3:45 in the morning and Dr. Riley was on duty. He was a younger doctor advancing quickly in the medical field. He monitored the floor every so often, walking past all of the patient rooms doing his rounds. The doctor was two rooms away from David's. Every time he was on the floor, he looked forward to seeing David. David was young, not even old enough to truly understand the real meaning of life. The doctor felt bad for him because he, too, was young, and the way he grew up was totally different. He opened David's door and walked inside, scanning the patient chart that contained all of his information. Dr. Riley checked all of the fluids that ran through his IVs. As he started checking David's pulse, he noticed something was different. He removed his glasses from his face and placed them down on the counter.

He was ecstatic and very happy to see what he'd just witnessed. Dr. Riley called in all of the other teams of doctors and nurses who were handling David's care. They all stood there watching and waiting to see what would happen next. David's eyes started to open, his fingers beginning to wiggle as he gripped the sheets of his bed, and they all cheered as David came back to life.

It had been an hour since David had been out of his coma; the doctors were surprised he made a full recovery. Normally, after receiving those types of blows to the head, the person would never make it out of the coma or there would be side effects, like extreme loss of memory and having to learn basic things all over again. David was built like a machine; always war ready, but the human body can be a mystery when dealing with issues of the brain. While David was in the coma, the doctors gave him the medications needed to treat his virus. He was much healthier than before. His hair was longer, his eyes were whiter, and his weight picked up. The doctors informed David that he had a strong immune system and his body took well to the medications.

"Hey there, young man. While you were out, we kept you under close observation. We watched how your body reacted to the medications and, I must say, you are doing better than we could ever have imagined. Your body healed faster than the average person; you can attribute that to your youth. So pretty much what I am saying to you is, you have another chance at life, young man. Take care of yourself and don't give up, because you can live a long, healthy life, longer than most HIV patients," the doctor stated.

The doctor patted him on the back and walked out of the room. David listened, but was not really fully aware of what he was talking about. He'd lost partial memory—he didn't know his name, how old he was, or where he was born. He looked down at his feet, wondering why he was shackled. He didn't know why he was in a coma or why he had war scars on his face and head. Frustrated for not being able to remember who he was, all he had was his inmate badge showing his picture, and a name that said correctional facility over the top. David demanded answers and was screaming at the doctors.

"Hey, Doc, what the hell is going on? Why am I shackled, where are these scars from, and who am I?" David questioned.

"So you don't remember anything at all?" the doctor asked.

"No, I don't," David replied.

The doctor excused himself, realizing now that David had lost some of his memory. David was scheduled to be extradited back to Dauphin County Prison that morning. They had to postpone his discharge date from the hospital in order to do more tests on him to see the severity of his condition. They had to test for Motor Neuron Disease, organ failure, and he needed to be evaluated for any mental illnesses.

After a month of testing and prodding, David was starting to feel better. He suffered from some short-term memory loss. The medical team wanted to keep David until the majority of his memory came back, then they would have to release him back to the prison. The doctors gave him as much information as they possibly could. They told him his health situation, his name, and that he was attacked in the county prison. The more they told David, the more he became confused as he tried to gain his memory back. Physically, David was the healthiest and strongest he had ever been in his life.

David got off the bed and looked in the mirror, touching the healed scars on his face and head. Thoughts slowly came back as he started remembering little by little. Anger possessed his mind as he remembered being surrounded by his enemy, thinking, *I'm a kill them motherfuckers*! Flashbacks of his once life was zooming through his mind a hundred miles a second. Faces of the people he killed, faces of his enemies, and the faces of his foster parents. When Danielle and the baby came across his mind, David put two fingers to his forehead, deep in thought. Pain came to his heart and tears filled his eyes as he vomited onto the floor. Danielle's face was all that appeared—the love of his world, his unborn child. David knew she would be worried sick; it had been months since he heard her voice. The thing that worried him most was did she have HIV or not? David grabbed a napkin and wiped his face off, then rinsed his mouth out with Listerine.

The sheriffs were there to extradite him back to the county jail. David stood on his two feet as the sheriffs escorted him out of his room. As he walked past all of the doctors, they smiled and waved, saying their goodbyes. During the time he was in the hospital, the nurses and doctors grew close to him and were happy he recovered.

When David was back at Dauphin County Prison (DCP), he received word from his attorney, Mr. Price, that there wasn't enough evidence to charge him for the York shootout. David's lawyer was on his side when he found out that his client was in a coma from a horrible jail attack. When his lawyer saw the news about David's girlfriend killing herself, it touched his heart. He could only imagine the heartache and suffering one young boy could fathom. From the police putting out in public news that David was infected with HIV, to Danielle committing suicide, the more Mr. Price went over his notes and began thinking to himself.

Brian was the best at this law game. He was witty, charming, and all the judges and DA's were his buddies. They played golf, attended bowling leagues, and their children all played for the same baseball teams. The first thing that came to his mind was a lawsuit, thinking, *this young man is going to be able to sue the city's socks off.* Brian was handling his case the whole time he was comatose, making a deal with the Dauphin County District Attorneys' office. All he needed was David to make it out of his coma, so he could sign the deal. David was sentenced to one to two years in a state prison facility with six months served. He beat the gun charge with Smooth at the Waffle House, so he would only be doing a short bid for the eight ball of crack cocaine found in his jeans. With everything he'd been through, through every ounce of blood that he'd spilled, David was still a child of God. God knew the pressures forced upon him and that he didn't have a chance since the beginning of life.

David was still on medical watch and, as much as he wanted to go to population, he couldn't. He was overcoming his short term memory loss; every day that passed, more of his memory emerged from the blackness. It was nine o'clock in the morning when David walked down the tier, thinking, *please, please, please pick up the phone.* David was on med block waiting for the state bus to come take all of the inmates to Camp Hill Prison that had been sentenced. The med block was much sweeter, cleaner, than the rest of the jail. The guards were much more lenient and the nurses weren't the average old grandmas with white hair. David picked up the phone and dialed Danielle's number, listening as it rung three times before there was an answer. When the phone call was accepted, a big smile came upon his face, knowing it had to be Danielle because her mother would never have answered the phone.

"Danielle," David said.

"No, this isn't Danielle; Danielle is dead, and don't you ever call here again. She killed herself all because of you. She hung herself from the window seal leaving only a death note. You gave my baby HIV and she killed herself. Fuck you, motherfucker, and go to hell where you belong. You're the child of Satan!"

Danielle's mother hung up the phone, crying. As bad as she hated to be this way, she couldn't help it. David had taken everything from her. Her love of the Lord could not secede the rage she held for David. Danielle's mother had been self-medicating since the death of her daughter, consuming alcohol and large doses of Xanax. She couldn't take it anymore, so after the funeral she planned to pack up her granddaughter and move back to Atlanta with family.

After Danielle's mother hung up the phone, David couldn't believe what he heard. Going by the tone of her voice he knew she was telling the truth about Danielle's suicide. David's body filled with anger as he slammed the phone against the hammer till it broke.

He dropped the phone, screaming at the top of his lungs, *"NO, no, no, what have I done?"* David was hysterical, not knowing what to think if the baby was dead or alive. Through his cold heart, through his cold soul, there was a weak spot, and Danielle was it. David went straight to his room and tried mercilessly to hold in the tears that needed release. Inside of his single man cell, he laid on his bed. He couldn't believe she would kill herself and the baby. He was devastated and overcome with grief.

CHAPTER 16

UNTHINKABLE

The pressure's on

A month had passed since the funeral, and Danielle's mother was all packed up and ready to move back down south. She had all of her furniture, clothes, and valuables loaded into a U-Haul truck. Christine was going to sell the house, but figured she could rent it out for now. She could use the extra $1,050 dollars a month while she got back on her feet in Atlanta.

It was her last day living in PA. Christine couldn't wait to leave. Her game plan was to get the baby and get a head start on the highway while she

1

still had daylight. It would be dark by the time she reached Virginia, so she planned to get a room and rest up near the town of Richmond. The next day she planned to drive straight to Atlanta, Georgia, just herself and her beautiful brand new granddaughter.

While Danielle's mother was at the hospital that afternoon, one of King's cousins was there visiting family with her boyfriend from York. She knew the situation with Danielle; King and everyone knew that Danielle was pregnant with David's baby. So when she called King, she informed him that Danielle killed herself and the baby survived. King immediately went into thought mode, still wanting revenge as if it was yesterday. King wanted David dead and would do anything to make sure that it happened! King thought to himself, *an eye for an eye, motherfucker. Yo' ass is mine now! Your bitch already offed herself, doing the job for me. Now I'm a take her mom's life and the life of the baby, too!*

Danielle's mother stood in her kitchen taking one last look around the place she once called home. All of her family in Atlanta was waiting for their arrival. The baby was asleep in the car seat, bundled up in blankets ready for the long drive.

Christine grabbed the keys to her rental truck off the fireplace when she heard short breaths. She walked down the hallway and, out of nowhere, two masked men grabbed her. One guy placed his gun against her heart while the other one put his hands around her throat. Danielle's mother was petrified, so scared that her only reaction was to knee him in the balls. The guy holding the gun fell to his knees holding his crotch; yet still he had a firm grasp on her leg as she kicked and squirmed to escape. The other guy grabbed her by the hair and smacked her with the back of his hand, so hard that she went flying, landing on the hardwood polished floor. The guy that Christine kneed in the nuts was coming back to his senses and he was more enraged than before.

As Christine tried to crawl to safety, the guy she hit stood over top of her and kicked her in the ribs. Blood spewed from her mouth onto the floor. He then took his gun and smacked her across the temple, knocking her out cold. They quickly went into action tying her up nice and tight, making sure she was restrained. When they went through her belongings, they saw she was relocating to Georgia. This was the perfect murder. They figured they would drive her somewhere close to Virginia, execute her, and then leave her dead in her car. They wanted to make it look like a murder/kidnapping. The police would think the baby was in the Virginia area.

"Say, bra, for real for real we can just finish it right here."

"Yea, that shit is too risky driving with her in the trunk and then the baby!"

"Let's kill her now, chop her up, and take her to the farm in Lancaster. Big Tony got a plug up there, we can feed her to the hogs. That's where big bra takes all of his bodies."

"Aight, fuck it then, it sounds like a plan to me. Lancaster right up the highway, and we can be done with this shit in less than two hours. First call King and see what he say. I'm trying to catch the let out downtown tonight. I heard it supposed to be crazy. They said last week them hill cats stomped the young boy out, put him in the ambulance all crazy." They both laughed.

When they walked inside the room, Danielle's mother acted like she was still out cold. She realized she was tied up with silver duct tape, thinking, *they're going to kill me* she began to panic.

The two goons sent by King started screwing the silencers on their guns, in preparation to take an innocent woman's life. As they were getting ready to send Christine to her maker, someone rang the doorbell. They were both startled, not knowing who it could be.

"Go see what's going on, bra."

One of the men tiptoed across the kitchen, so he could peek through the window and get a better view. As he got closer to the door, the doorbell rang again. He kneeled down lower, looking out of the side curtain. It was a Spanish woman in her early forties holding a bundle of roses and a going away card. She was trying to say her last goodbyes. The Spanish lady was still ringing the doorbell, being very adamant about coming inside. When she tried opening the door, the men knew they had trouble and they had to do something fast.

"What should we do? I'm not trying to kill this bitch, too. Shit will be too hot, bra."

"Man, fuck that, bra. It's no love for none of these motherfuckers. We have to kill her, too."

As the guy was getting ready to open the door and spray the Spanish lady's brains against the side of the house, she placed the flowers and card down onto the porch and walked away. She had no idea, no clue, that she was a second away from meeting her maker. The coast was clear as they walked back inside of the room where Christine was.

"Oh shit, where the fuck she go?"

They both started searching the house, as one said, "She couldn't have made it far, bra, and she's hiding somewhere."

They searched and searched, not knowing she was right beneath their noses hiding under the table. Danielle's mother had awakened while they were at the door. She crawled beneath the table, hiding and praying that they wouldn't find her. The baby was still in her car seat fast asleep. Devunyae had been fed a whole bottle, so she knew she would sleep for at least three hours.

The two men became frustrated, losing hope. "She must have ran out the back. Grab the baby, we out, G." They grabbed the car seat and speed-walked out of the back door.

When Danielle's mother realized they were taking the baby, she knew she had to stop them. She crawled from under the table, trying with all her might to get their attention. She began kicking the chairs from under the table in an attempt to make noise. They couldn't hear her as they continued walking out of the back door. All she could hear was the screen door slam behind them.

Danielle's mother couldn't get untangled from the ropes fast enough to stop them. They walked the baby out the back door as if nothing ever happened! Christine managed to get loose from the ropes and duct tape. Still kind of dizzy from the attack, she stumbled and fell into the flat screen TV, knocking over the DVD player and cable box. She ran out of the door screaming, in full panic mode, asking for help.

The neighbors heard the screams coming from outside of their homes. They all started coming out of their houses to see what was going on. Knowing the past drama that had occurred at the Bradshaw residence before, all the neighbors became overprotective. They were always watching and stopping by to make sure she was okay.

"Help, help! They kidnapped my grandbaby." She ran to one of her neighbors and used their telephone to call the police. "Hello, please, somebody help me. I need police at 2331 Huntington Lane—my granddaughter has just been kidnapped."

The operator was trying to keep her calm, asking her questions, getting vital information. Christine felt as if the operator was taking too long, when they had only seconds to spare. Time was of the essence.

Christine dropped the phone and ran outside, getting into her car. She pressed on the gas not, knowing she had put the car in reverse, and unintentionally slammed into the car behind her. She put her car in drive, frantically pulling off, weaving in and out of traffic while looking left to right. They were only a couple of minutes ahead of her, so she knew they couldn't have gone far. She was speeding down the street, driving recklessly, not caring if she crashed or killed herself. Just as she was about to turn on to Market Street, she took a swift glance right and saw the two men in the car.

They were stopped at the red light in a black Ford club wagon. She didn't know what to do or how she was going to do it—all she knew was that she had to save the baby, Devunyae. She figured she would follow them to see where they were taking her Grandchild and then call the police. She started tailing them two cars back, keeping her head low, hoping not to be spotted.

The two goons hired by King were veterans of the streets; looking in their mirrors or behind their backs was normal everywhere they went. They turned a few corners, keeping their gaze in their side mirrors to see if anyone trailed them.

They stopped in the middle of the street when they noticed a familiar face. Both of them got out of the car and started moving toward Christine. When she saw they were onto her, she panicked and started backing up, but her already fractured bumper got stuck on a parked car.

Christine threw the shaft into reverse then into drive, nothing would work—she couldn't get the car out. She began to shiver, knowing her life was about to come to an end. The two men drew their weapons as they walked to her car. She began sobbed and prayed silently. She did not want to die. The two men locked eye to eye, both nodding in submission, ready to terminate their initial target. Just as they were getting ready to squeeze the trigger, sirens echoed loudly.

"What should we do, bra?"

"It's your lucky day, woman," one of the men said.

He tapped his friend on the arm for them to leave. They didn't want to jeopardize getting caught, so they turned around, running toward their truck, and sped off. Christine had never been more scared in her life. She was breathing hard, trying to catch her breath and relax her body, so that her heart would calm down. The men pulled off with the baby and into the sunset. The cops arrived within seconds and began searching the entire city for Devunyae. Her Amber Alert cluttered the airwaves, plastering her picture on the news, social sites, and along all the major highways.

CHAPTER 17

NU-NU

Twisted Morals

D avid was lying down on his bunk bed in a daze, staring at the ceiling. When a C.O. stopped at his door, David thought, *what the fuck is this about*?

The C.O. spoke, "David, you have mail, bud, here you go." The C.O. handed David a thick wad of mail and he reached out and grabbed it. After having the feeling of no one in his corner for years he was stunned to receive such a magnitude of mail. David didn't get one, two, or three letters—he had received nine. Sitting up on his bed, he started going through the letters. David prayed that there was a letter from Danielle. He wanted to believe what her mother had told him was simply a hateful lie, but there was no letter. David opened every piece of mail. There were two letters from his grandfather, a letter from Molt in Pittsburgh, and six letters from Poca. His grandfather had been trying to reach out to him after doing fifteen years in a federal prison. He was living out in Chicago working at a post office trying to earn an honest living. He told David that he loved him and wanted him to come to the Midwest with him. He sent David a few pictures of himself and David's mother Elektra. David stared at his mother's picture for hours, wishing he'd met her at least one time. She was beautiful, gorgeous, and her smile was the prettiest he'd ever seen. After living life convinced he didn't have any family, it was an emotional relief that someone out there was a blood relative. The sheer fact that they loved and wanted to get to know him gave David a feeling of hope. David grabbed Molt's letter and opened it.

I pray this letter finds you in good health, as for me I'm on my same shit. You know shit been hectic for a pimp out here! Somebody killed my sister, them dirty ass feds found her decomposing in a trunk. She had twenty-six holes in her body, no fingers, no toes, only way they knew it was her was by her teeth bra. They found her out Cleveland with half a pool stick up her ass four months ago. I'm still sick about that shit. She was fucking with this crab nicca heavy in that weight game. Knowing her she must've done robbed the nicca. Her friend Keisha said it was for thirty grand and two kilos of heroin. You know niccaz not letting that ride, retaliation gone be extra you feel me?

Molt was devastated about his sister. David thought, *what the fuck, how she get caught slipping like that?* David had no room for sympathy after hearing that his love killed herself; it was like throwing stones at a brick wall. David cared about Nu-Nu. She was a thorough bitch, a Ryder for real. He was hurt, but his heart bled too much blood for it to be affected. David's memory was starting to fully come back, but some things were still a blur. He remembered the conversation he had with the detectives and how they were on the hunt for Nu-Nu. He knew now they had no evidence, no connection, or way to charge him with the murder of Smooth.

Lastly, David opened the letters from Poca. "Oh shit, how she find me?" David opened the letters in all smiles, reading through each and every last one of them.

This was the biggest smile David had shown in a while, as he imagined her face right in front of his eyes. He never thought in a million years that he would ever see or hear from her again. She sent him pictures of old flicks they had taken before she left for California.

Poca always loved David. Her heart crumbled into a thousand pieces when she had to relocate from Pennsylvania. Poca still loved him, never forgetting their connection, their bond—they were just right for each other.

Poca wanted David to come to California once he was released. She never knew what happened to David. She called one of her friends from PA to see if she'd seen or heard anything. Her friend told her the last thing she heard was that he was killing and robbing everybody. She told Poca David was wanted for murder and all types of other shit. She did her homework online, calling the surrounding prisons in an attempt to get information on his whereabouts. When she found out he was being held in the county prison, she got the address and began sending him letters every week in the hopes that he would respond. Poca was living out in California, still hiding from the Spanish mafia, still hustling, still on her shit. Poca, the real hustle girl no matter where she went, where she ended up, she would make something pop!

CHAPTER 18

PICTURE LUST

Man's best friend

D avid tried not to think of his past and present demons. He was lying on his bed looking at the pictures of Poca, gazing at how gorgeous, exhilarating, and magnificent she still was. He felt a bit guilty for the flutter she gave his heart. Poca knew what drove Davi1d wild, the poses and positions in which she took her photos was enough to drive any man insane. In each photo Poca made different sexual faces that she knew David would yearn for, trying to remind him of times when he was deep inside her stroking, working it, stretching her love tunnel.

David was becoming aroused, reminiscing on the last time that he had seen her. The last time he felt her walls, her tightness, how loud she would moan in Spanish. Poca was David's heart, hustle queen, his real lover as well as best friend. When he saw the one picture of her in this La Pearl lingerie, with her body showing just enough, he went crazy. Poca wore a purple bustier and some white boy shorts. You could see the thickness and definition in her shorts, fitting her perfectly. She had a tattoo of David's name above her heart. Poca was a fashion icon who was always coordinating, making sure everything matched. Her eye lashes were purple and her lip gloss shiny, with a sprinkle of purple glitter all over her body. This made her appear as if she was magical.

David hadn't had any sort of sexual activity in months. He started thinking of times when he used to punish her. No matter how deep inside of her he went or how much he stretched her walls out, Poca still allowed him to fuck her. He used to make her squat on his face, while he licked and sucked her clitoris until she came. She would give him head in the weirdest places: elevators, the mall dressing rooms, and always, in the car. David missed every bit of her, almost forgetting their bond until he read her letters and looked at her pictures.

David sat on the edge of his bed with a hard on bulging out of his shorts. In deep thought, David suddenly laughed and smiled, finding it hilarious of the time when he was hitting it from the back and Poca started screaming and squirting, splashing juices, and some landed in his left eye.

He was more than aroused now. Getting up from his bed, he grabbed the lotion from off the counter and a towel, placing it over top of the door to cover the window. David poured the lotion into the palm of his hand and covered his penis with it. He held the pictures of Poca, mesmerized by her sexual appeal. He slowly massaged his penis, going up and down imagining the feeling of her warm, tight pussy. He could feel the sensations of each stroke every time he rubbed the tip of his penis. David was in deep thought, different sexual scenes from Brandy to Cream all racing through his brain. Getting closer to his final destination, David sped up the pace. His toes were beginning to clench looking like they were throwing gang signs'. His knees started locking and his hand was beginning to get fatigued. David tilted his head back as he got ready to climax, knowing it was going to be a big one; he could feel it passing through his knees. David's whole body clenched as he released a large amount sperm, exploding everywhere.

Feeling relieved after getting the sexual frustration out of his system, David kissed the picture of Poca and got off of his bed. He walked to the sink, grabbing the soap and a rag. He let the water get warm and began cleaning himself off. When he finished drying off, he laid down on the bed and fell asleep like a baby.

Seven days later, David was on his way to court to be sentenced to a one to two year prison term in a state facility, with no possible chance of early release. He met with his lawyer before seeing the Judge. He was credited for the six months that he was incarcerated in Dauphin County Prison. Through all the bullshit you'd think David would be grateful he made it out of those murder charges, but he wasn't. He walked away with a one to two year bid. That was a slap on the wrist for David, and not nearly enough to make him change his ways. Now on his way to Camp Hill State Prison, where the big dogs go, where everyone from Pennsylvania: Pittsburgh, Harrisburg, Reading, Chester, and Philadelphia must go to be classified before being shipped to their home Prison. This was where the murderers, rapists, cartels, and everyone who pretty much didn't give a fuck went.

David was on the twenty-five minute bus ride headed toward Camp Hill Prison. He wasn't worried or concerned at all, being twenty pounds bigger and the strongest he'd ever felt in his life. As all of David's memories came back, his heart beat harder and harder by the second. David thought to himself, *Smooth is dead, Danielle is dead, my baby is dead, Cream, Portia, Nu-Nu, my Mom, my Dad, every motherfucking body is dead!* David was crazy insane with nothing to live for, but he knew he still had to play things smart. State prison was a different ball game. Thinking, *I'm getting me a shank from the rip. I dare one of these busters test me if I'm stabbing everything moving?* This is the first time in years David was free of drugs; his thoughts were accurate, making him able to see things much clearer. The bus finally pulled up in front of Camp Hill State Prison, which was much larger than the county.

David and thirty other inmates all got out of their seats and walked off of the bus. The C.O.s instructed them to line up on the bus side by side, so they could take count. An older inmate stood in back of David, determined to cause trouble his first day and not wanting to follow the orders made by the C.O.s. He was tall and slim, with a bald, white head. He had lightning bolts tatted on both sides of his neck.

"Fuck you, hillbilly corn eating motherfuckers, I ain't doing shit," yelled the cocky inmate.

The C.O. swiftly taking authority, took his Billy club and struck the man on the side of his legs twice speed balling him to the hole. This was the first time David had been inside of a state prison. He took a glance at all the other inmates, seeing that some were old, some were young, some White and Hispanic, but the majority were black. David already had a game plan in his mind, which was to hit the yard and work out. He didn't want any friends, he didn't want to speak to anyone—"fuck the world" was his motto. David and the rest of the inmates all walked in a single file line headed inside of the prison. They all had to get naked, bend over, and cough to make sure they weren't bringing any illegal drugs or weapons inside the prison. They had to shower with this gel that would kill lice, crabs, or any other bugs a human could carry. Once they all finished showering and getting changed into their blue or brown prison suits, they were ready to go to classification. David was giving his information to an older white lady assigned to registering inmates when she asked him a troubling question

"Where do you want your body to be shipped if you were to die?" It startled him, thinking, *this shit must be real up here!* He gave her his information and kept it moving. At Camp Hill there were two type of inmates, you had your "Blues" and your "Browns." The Blues were the inmates who were being classified and shipped off to another prison. The Browns were inmates who were classified and would remain at Camp Hill State Prison.

David was classified to Camp Hill Prison as his home jail. They figured since his time was short he might as well stay there and finish his time. David was pleased with working in the kitchen, as it was one of the best jobs in prison, and the gravest. You can eat as much as you want, so David quickly went from one hundred and fifty pounds to one hundred and ninety pounds in seven months. He worked out every day, running the track every morning, hitting that steel. He was solid like a rock, ripped, bulking up quickly with a bench press of three hundred pounds. He was determined to go back to Harrisburg a gorilla in full force as he finished out his war with King. David was eating good, working in the kitchen, taking his medications daily, and reading books. His hair was back to braids, but not as long as they used to be.

He sat in his cell writing his grandfather and Brandy. He'd already informed Poca he would love to come out to California and see her. She sent him pictures of the beach, palm trees, and candy painted low rider cars. David had never been to the west coast or to the beach before, so in his eyes it seemed like a Gangster's playground. The first thing he thought was how no one would know who he was, so he could rob everything out that bitch and come back home with his money right. David had a couple recent pictures of himself; he knew she'd be amazed at how big he'd gotten.

He read the letter his grandfather had sent him and decided to put him on his visitation list. His grandfather kept insisting that once released he should come to Chicago and start a new beginning and, as soon as the weather broke, he was coming to see David. As he started reading Brandy's letter, he already knew what she was going to say.

Brandy poured her heart out, saying things like *I know you killed my brother everyone is saying it*, but a part of her didn't want to believe it. Brandy couldn't find it in her heart to think that David would kill his own brother. He didn't even respond to Brandy's letter, thinking *fuck her and Smooth.*

He got through his prison bid by reading and working out. All day he did push-ups, sit ups, and work. He never spoke to anyone. People tried to start conversations with him, but he'd look them in the eye and just ignore them. David's time was short, and he wasn't planning on being there too long; he figured *I'm in and out, fuck these niccaz.*

David kept a frown on his face from the day he walked in, showing no signs of weakness. David remembered when Smooth and Big O would have conversations about the differences in the county jails and state prison. From their conversation there were only a few things that stuck out to David. One was that you had to be hard; two, stay to yourself; and, lastly, never tell anyone how much time you're doing.

CHAPTER 19

WANTED DEAD

A price to pay

David minded his own business and never indulged in anything that didn't involve him. Inmates from Harrisburg would converse about stories from the streets, who was fucking who, who ratting, who getting all of the money, and who was terrorizing out there. They talked about David in all of the jails. He knew King would eventually find out his location and try to have him murdered.

Word had already spread throughout the jails before David arrived. King was a made man, big homey, boss, having respect all throughout Pennsylvania. Pittsburgh, Philly, Erie, all the made men in those areas loved and respected King. King wanted David dead; wanted his blood line wiped out completely. King called every boss in PA; the price on David's head was as high as Mount Everest. When word got out that it was a mega hit on David, even the guards were tempted. Every lifer, every killer, along with some of the guards, all wanted David's head. Everyone tried to get their greedy hands on the hit money before the next. They knew David was a killer, a goon, the only man that ever warred with King and lived. They knew who David was; the gangsters from Pittsburgh and Philly heard about the work he was putting in. They all respected his gangster, his mob boy cadence, all wanting to show him love, but the price was too overwhelming. All of the older inmates liked David, even though there was a hit out on him and, at any moment, there could be an attack.

David was one of the youngest inmates in the prison, a juvenile tried as an adult. The older inmates liked that he was mature for his age and stayed to himself instead of socializing or fraternizing with any inmates. Anytime an inmate tried to be his friend, he took it as if they were trying to set him up. David was under pressure, paranoid, looking over his shoulders, knowing someone would try to take him out. Prison was like the streets: if you well respected, you well connected. It's nothing to have access to knives, drugs, and cell phones. David heard the gay stories before, but never witnessed this many men having sex with men. The gay dudes were very flamboyant, wearing makeup, walking around like they were better than females. They had the walk down pat, switching, walking like runway models with perfect posture. Gay men in prison were the happiest because jail was paradise for them. They could get dick all day and night, selling their bodies for cheap dollars.

David was on the pull up bars doing ten sets of twenty, making pull ups look easy. Every time he pulled himself up you could see the cuts in the muscles of his back like a Spartan. He finished his workout sweating, out of breath, wiping his face with a brown towel. A gay Spanish man walked over to him switching, with his hands on his waist and chewing bubble gum.

"Hey, handsome, can me and my bitch braid your hair? We would make you look delicious for your visit. Both of us together, we will have you up and out and ready for yard in no time."

All the inmates with braids or dread locks got their hair twisted by the gay men. David didn't trust them at all, thinking, *these motherfuckers trying to get that hit bread*!

"Fa sho, how much is it?" David said.

"Five for me and five for my bitch."

"Aight, say no more. Y'all better not fuck my shit up, or I ain't paying nothing."

David didn't trust a soul, already having it in his head that this was a set up. He figured he'd let them be his first example to show the prison he ain't playing games. He went to his cell, grabbing his whack just in case the two men got out of line. David told them to meet him at his cell; in no way was he considering going to theirs.

They waited outside until he gave them the okay to enter. They walked inside and David sat on the table, combing his hair out. The gay men brought their own grease and accessories. David was observing them and noticed their combs were sharp at the bottom and could be used as a weapon. The two men started braiding his hair, twisting and weaving as if they worked at an African hair shop.

They both started acting weird and nervous, and David picked up on their shady vibes instantly. They continued braiding David's hair, almost finishing the job. He watched their every move. The Black gay guy looked at the Spanish guy, alerting him that he was getting ready to make his move. He took the comb and stabbed it into David's shoulder. David being much bigger and stronger, took the comb and stabbed the black man in his chest. The other guy tried to stab David in his back. David moved out of the way, throwing a ferocious upper cut to break the guy's nose with one punch. He lifted him by his legs and power drove him head first to the floor. He pulled the whack from out of the black guy and started stabbing both of them multiple times.

"Yeah motherfucker, you thought you could catch me slipping, oh, so ya'll thought y'all was going to take me out." The two men were both screaming, bleeding profusely, and trying to get out of David's cell. David had their whack and his whack; they were backed into the corner of his cell without any weapon. They had to get through him to get out.

David's body became weaker due to the loss of blood he sustained from his shoulder wound. He swung the whack, missing the black guy who luckily slipped away, running out of the cell and leaving the Spanish guy for dead. David jumped on top of the Spanish guy, standing over top of him, and continued to stab him in multiple areas. The Spanish guy was in bad shape, bleeding from a major artery, dying slowly.

C.O.'s started running inside the cell, snatching David off of him and then restraining him.

"Yeah, motherfuckers straight like that," David yelled as they drug him to seclusion. The Spanish guy lay dead in the corner of David's cell, holding his stomach. The C.O.s rushed him to the infirmary before he bled out all over the prison floors. They see inmates get killed all the time, so their only concern was that they didn't want to clean up all that blood. They speed balled David to the hole, dragging him by his feet and arms.

"Get off me, motherfucker. They came in my cell trying to rape me. It was they whack not mine, I just defended myself. Look, they stabbed me in my shoulder. I'm bleeding, motherfucker."

David was in the hole for three months, but wasn't charged for the murder. The judge ruled it self-defense because the two inmates attacked him in his cell. He was over his minimum. David knew that even though he didn't get charged, the parole board would still give him a hit. To make a long story short, he comprehended that he was going to max his sentence out.

David got out of the hole ten pounds lighter and ready to get back into his heavy workout mode. After three months of nothing but pushups, sit ups, and stretching, he was cut up like a bag of dope. They sent David back to the same block, not caring if his life was still in jeopardy. David didn't care either, feeling unstoppable, unbreakable, and knowing he was merely months to freedom.

It was Friday morning and Danielle's birthday. David was preparing to go to the yard. He put on his boots, grabbed his sweater, and started walking out of the cell. He really never stayed in the pod because working out would keep his mind clear and the pain would go away. It kept the thought of dying outside of his mind.

He was in a depressed mood because of Danielle's birthday, so he decided to stay in the pod. He walked down the tier and sat in front of the T.V. There was no one else in the pod, everyone either left for yard or was still asleep in their cells. David grabbed the remote and started flicking through the channels, thinking, *I haven't watched TV in months.*

As David was flicking through the channels, he saw a commercial about HIV. His depressed mood switched to anger immediately. He did not need to be reminded that he was a dead man walking. He turned the channel, trying his hardest not to release a tear. He continued turning through the channels and stopped at 106 and Park. They were playing an old school Scarface song, *Never Seen a Man Cry Till I Seen a Man die.* David looked up to Scarface as one of his hood heroes. So David turned the volume up and enjoyed his song, bopping his head to the bass of the beat. David was relaxing, chilling, and happy to be out of the hole.

When he noticed an older OG walking toward him with his chess board, he thought *what the fuck is wrong with this old head?* The OG pimp sat down across from David and laid the chess board down on top of the table. He then started setting up the pieces, looking at David as if he challenged him to play a game of chess. David played chess a couple times with Smooth when he was younger, but didn't understand the true meaning behind the great game.

"What you know about chess, little pimp? Do you know that this game is the meaning of life? Every move, every step that you make in life should be thought three steps ahead, and the same rules apply in chess. So let me ask you again, have you ever played chess?"

At first David wasn't paying him too much attention, but when he started speaking knowledge, he caught David's attention. David read 48 Laws of Power and the Art of War, so he was into strategizing, elements of surprise; a thinker, no question.

"Yea, I played a few times. I'm alright. That was some real shit you said, though, bra!" David said.

"Come play me a game, little pimp. Let me see where your mind is at."

David decided to play the OG in a few games of chess, and found he actually enjoyed playing chess and talking to the OG. As time passed, David and the OG began playing chess more and more. The OG was dropping jewels, knowledge, and game for the hoes on David like a father to a son. The OG liked David, considering he was a young boy in state prison. David was becoming a great chess player fast; he understood the three step rules to life and applied them to the chessboard. David was soaking up all of the knowledge that the OG was giving him, becoming stronger, smarter, and hungrier. This was the hungriest he'd ever been in his life.

David was still hitting the yard, running the track, focusing a little more on his cardio. He wrote Poca back and forth, telling her he was maxing out and was close to his home date. Poca told David if he moved out to California he could live with her, she had her own apartment and vehicles. David worked out twice as much, knowing he was getting ready to be released from state prison. He was now two-hundred and fifty pounds solid, standing at 6'2, tall like his father. He bench pressed three hundred to 385 pounds and could do thirty pull ups at one time.

He was doing his daily workout when a guy from Philly approached him. He was about forty pounds bigger than David. David hated to be interrupted in the middle of a workout, but continued working out, sweating, breathing hard, and grunting every time he lifted the fifty pound dumbbell.

"Say, my nicca. I need them fifty pound dumbbells. You been holding them things down for the last half hour, dog," the Philly guy said.

David dropped the weights. Taking off his black glasses, David walked closer to the man and rolled up the sleeves of his shirt. David's face showed no mercy, no fear, no respect, and he looked at him with a stare of death.

"I don't think you know me, bra. You see me using them, what's this a "G" check? How you gone check a gangster with a cemetery in his back yard?" David said

The inmate from Philly was a lifer; he received a letter from one of his folks. There was a fifty thousand dollar hit on David's head. The lifer needed the money for his family back home; his mother didn't have insurance and was dying from a liver infection. So it was a no brainer to David that he was there to collect.

The lifer had been thinking for months now how he could hit David due to the fact that he was such a hard person to hit. The lifer already did his homework, seeing that David was a killer like him. He walked over to David, asking him if he could use the weights just to see how he would respond. If David had given him the weights, he planned to grab the weight and hit David on the side of his head with it, then slit his throat.

Philly inmates overpopulated the prisons, being the biggest city in Pennsylvania. To Philly they were the only city popping in Pennsylvania, the only city getting money, and the only city on that gangster shit. So when they came across a 110 percent nicca out of Harrisburg, lifers, trappers, and stone cold killers would embrace him to brotherhood. That was many years ago now. Harrisburg is a power house name in any state prison in Pennsylvania.

"Nah, my boy. I'm just fucking with you. I heard you about that lifestyle are you Muslim?" the lifer asked

"What the fuck you talking about? You don't know me. Dudes want me dead, bra. I aint got no love for nobody in this bitch!" David said.

The lifer was older, so he knew to keep calm and not react; he only wanted to feel David out.

"Calm down, cuz, I got three bodies in my backyard to my nicca. I'm from North Philly serving two life sentences. I'm never going home. This is my world now, feel me, and I only fuck with niccaz like me. Either you're Muslim on your dean or a killer like me," the lifer said.

David was becoming agitated and getting angrier by the second. David automatically took it as if he was coming to kill him. His hands started getting sweaty, his heart started beating and his thoughts were racing. David picked the weight back up as if he was about to start working out again. Before the Philly born lifer could say anything else, David swung the fifty pound dumbbell, hitting him on the side of his temple. The guy fell face first and fell with all his weight like a ton of bricks. David spit in his face as he stepped over top of him, as if nothing ever happened. The guy was lying on the ground, shaking with foam coming out of his mouth. His eyes rolled to the back of his head. David looked back, thinking *if he dies, he dies!* He was very paranoid and couldn't deal with people talking to him for too long and, after the incident with the gay guys, he damn sure wasn't going to ever be caught slipping again.

He was going to be out the door in a few months and couldn't wait to see the world again. He walked inside of his cell and laid down on his bed. One of the C.O.'s walked past and gave David his mail. It was a letter from Danielle's mother. When he saw her name on the letterhead, his belly filled with butterflies, thinking, *what the hell could she possibly have to say to me?*

David opened up the letter and started reading it. She told David that she was sorry for all the horrible things she'd said to him. She told him Danielle's last words, which were that she would be waiting for him at the crossroads. When she got to the point of the letter was when all hell in his mind would break loose. She told him that the baby was alive, surviving through the death of Danielle. When she told him that someone broke into her house and attacked her, then kidnapped the baby, David snapped! She sent a couple pictures of the baby, so he could at least see what baby Devunyae looked like. She was very small with jet black curly hair. She looked identical to David, she was his twin; her grandmother named her Devunyae.

As David was staring at his daughter's pictures, his body filled with anger, destruction, and a rage that he had never felt before. David was under the impression that his daughter was dead. He starting punching the walls, scarring his hands, and screamed at the top of his lungs as blood leaked from his knuckles. He had only a few months left, and his only thought process was, *I'm a kill every last one of them motherfuckers I swear to God.*

CHAPTER 20

DRINK AWAY

The pain shows

Christine departed Pennsylvania and migrated back to Atlanta, Georgia where she was originally from. Danielle's father resented her mother; hated her with everything in him. Tony told her that he wished she was dead for allowing this terrible thing to happen to his daughter. Christine couldn't take the guilt, especially after everything that had happened; she began to lose her sanity. She was not the same anymore since the abduction. She'd been admitted to a couple psychiatric hospitals. She tried swallowing pills, cutting her wrists, she even tried to crash her car into a light pole. One day she was going through it, not being able to look at

1

herself in the mirror. After it sank in that Danielle likely killed herself from the encouragement of her harsh words, Christine just couldn't handle that. She got into her vehicle on the passenger side. She grabbed a bottle of Seagram's gin and started guzzling it. Alcohol became her suppression for the pain. After she finished off the bottle of gin, she was well over the line of being intoxicated. She sat there with her head spinning like a tornado, talking to herself.

Danielle's father killed her with his words. "He hates me; he wishes that I was dead, everyone is blaming me, me, me."

She opened up the glove compartment and grabbed her bottle of psychiatric meds. She twisted the cap off and poured the pills into her hand as her mind was ready to end it all. She threw the pills in her mouth with barely any time to think, knowing this would end her life. Realizing what she was doing, and realizing she was not capable of ending her life, Christine quickly opened her eyes and spit the pills out of the window.

She knew she was in bad shape. Her family in Atlanta couldn't handle all her personal issues, so they decided to send her to a group home in Augusta, Georgia. As she slowly got herself back together, she hoped and prayed that her granddaughter was safe and alive. Every day she called, questioning the police to see if they had any leads. The feds, detectives, and all of the city cops were searching high and low for baby Devunyae. They still hadn't found any clues, or leads, and their investigation was hopelessly deadlocked.

King was still holding Devunyae captive, having his aunt aid and care for her. He was waiting patiently for David to be released from prison. He wanted revenge for the killing of Smooth and for him shooting him in the shoulder. King was strong and powerful, having multiple allies with the ability to touch anyone with just one phone call! He knew what type of person, savage, and hot boy he was warring with. David was a killer and would kill anyone with no regrets, no remorse, and no fear. He remembered when they tried to kill David at the hotel. When he looked in the rearview mirror as he tried to escape, he noticed David taking a cutter assault rifle from the dead cop. He started shooting mercilessly, knocking out one of the tires on King's car, making him crash. David ran over to him with the M 16 pointed at his chest. Right before he could squeeze the trigger, a cop shot him in the back. King witnessed the killer, the murderer, and the ghostly spirit in his eyes. King knew if it wasn't for the cop, David would have left his dick in the dirt. King had to kill David, or one day he would stare down the barrel of his gun biting the same bullet that Smooth bit.

David was furious, incapable of handling the horrible news he had just received. He was pacing back and forth in his cell, stressing. His plan was to get released and move out to California with Poca and start a new life, but now things had changed. Once he got the letter from Danielle's mother, he started contemplating if he should stick to the plan. He wanted to kill King, his sister, and his whole family. He would go to sleep thinking about killing him and didn't care if he lost his life trying. David knew the cops would never find his daughter. King would have females aiding the baby and treating her as if she was his own. King would never harm the baby; his only intention was to kidnap her and make David come to him.

David was steaming inside, the feeling being ten times more intense from when he went in. The time David served was not enough to change him; all it did was make him smarter, stronger, and more deadly. He was still attending church every Sunday, educating himself more about the Lord. He would never forget Pastor Tate in the short time that he knew him, remembering his words vividly as if they were spoken yesterday. He would send prayers to his Lord in a sealed envelope, with angels guiding it through heaven's doors. He would ask for forgiveness, safety, and direction to the road of redemption. He started loving church more and more. It gave him something to believe in besides revenge, heartbreak, and shame. The more he attended church, the more he realized the Lord was the only friend he needed. David never had a mother, father, or family; all he had was his own shadow. David's celly was on his dean, and prayed six times a day. David never heard of Allah or the Islamic faith, but after reading his celly's Quran it all made sense. David respected the Muslim brotherhood, the discipline, and their beliefs. The prison was eighty percent Muslim, being the fastest growing religion in the world.

David finished out the rest of his prison sentence infused in rage. It was too much for one man to fathom or embrace. David had a mission that needed to be completed: get his daughter back and murder King.

David was in his cell doing pushups, trying to make time fly, when a C.O. walked past, "Collins, get dressed. You have a visitor."

David had no idea he was getting a visit, so when the C.O. informed him he had a visit it caught him off guard. David thought, *a visit? I'm not getting no visit, these motherfuckers are trying to take my life!*

David finished doing two sets of pushups and got dressed; he brushed his teeth and quickly washed up at the sink. He walked out of his cell, looking left to right. The man whose head he'd split open hadn't died, so David knew one day he would retaliate. He expected retaliation in his line of work, never underestimating his adversary. David walked down the tier on his way to his visit, stopping at the desk where the pod officer was preparing his slip.

When he walked to the visiting room, he showed his slip to the officers and walked past them. This was the first visit David ever had in State Prison, so the visit thing was new to him. As David entered the visiting room, he looked around if wonder of who it could be, since he'd put only his Grandfather Frankie and Poca on his visiting list. So as he continued walking, he noticed a man standing in front of him, a man with the same face structure as him. David looked at him and tried to envision himself in a better place in life; he figured it had to be his grandfather. The closer he got, the more David was stunned. He couldn't believe how much they resembled each other. They walked over to each other, shook hands, and hugged. They sat down and stared at each other for what felt like hours.

"Damn, boy. What? You in here eating the weights, you big as a house! I finally get to meet my grandson, man; you know you got a big family out in

Chicago. They all can't wait to meet you. We all know what happened to your mom, I'm not sure what all you know, but..." David cut him off.

"What you mean what happened? Nah, I don't know nothing. All I have is one picture of my mother, that's it."

"Damn, that's crazy, so you don't know the story?"

"No, I don't. Tell me," David said.

"It all started with the passing of your grandmother, she died in a car accident. Your grandmother was one heck of a woman. We shared a daughter together, which was your mother. I ended up catching a case and went on the run from the law and eventually ended up doing fed time. So when your grandmother died, they sent our daughter to live with my brother in Pennsylvania. He started raping her over and over again till eventually she shot him to death. While she was in prison, she found out she was pregnant, and the baby inside of her stomach was to her, her very own uncle. While she was giving birth to you in prison, she died in her cell."

Confused, he shook his head, as a single tear trickled down his cheek. It was far too much to take in at one time,

"So you're telling me my uncle is my father? That I was born in a fucking cell? My mom was a killer, my dad was a rapist, and you did fifteen years fed time? That's crazy, pops, how one generation can affect the next. I didn't deserve this life. I was born in this shit. This answers a lot of my questions. Now it all makes sense. Damn, so I have cousins, aunties, and a grandfather. Why after all these years, lonely years, nobody came and looked for me?" David said.

"Listen, I don't have all the answers, grandson, but one thing I can tell you is you have family in the mid-west. Boy cousins, girl cousins, it's a bunch of them, and they all close to your age, man. I'm a send you pictures soon as I get home. Damn, you look like your father and mother. I miss both of them. So how is everything going? I see you're coming home soon. What are your plans? Are you going back to Pennsylvania? I know you was telling me that you had some troubles there. You can come to Chicago and stay with me if you want," Frankie said.

"That a be cool, but I have some unfinished business that I must handle first. Somebody kidnapped my daughter and I know who did it."

"Somebody kidnapped your daughter, what type of shit is that? Are the police looking for her? That is crazy! I know it's none of my business, but I think you should come home on a straight line. Let the police handle it!" Frankie said.

David didn't like the words that came out of his grandfather's mouth and his attitude immediately changed. David was already in severe rage, a hot head. When he found out his daughter was alive and had been kidnapped, it took his mind further into the darkness. At this point David didn't want any family, none of that sentimental bullshit. He wanted destruction, revenge; he hated the world and anyone who lived a happy life.

"What the fuck you mean let the cops handle it? These motherfuckers kidnapped my daughter and all you can say is let the cops handle it. Fuck that," David said.

Frankie had no idea, not a clue of what type of person his grandson was. All he knew was that he was his grandson and he was incarcerated. A C.O. walked by their area, making sure everything was okay. David stood up in silence. He really didn't want to go hard on his grandfather. He knew he was the last of his bloodline.

David gave his grandfather a hug, telling him: "I'm going to get in contact with you when the time is right. Right now my mind is in another place. I'm sorry for spazzing out on you, but my life is at a destructive point, so when I find my path and become settled, I will reach out to you, grandpop," David said.

Frankie was confused and didn't understand what just happened. He was shocked and wondering why his grandson just flipped out. Frankie was at peace with his life, changing his spirits during his incarceration. He stayed seated and watched as David walked away, leaving the visiting room. David went back to his cell and started writing Poca a letter. He told her his release date and that he was coming home straight to her.

CHAPTER 21

CALIFORNIA

A mafia's princess

P oca was now living on the west coast in Los Angeles, California, having to relocate due to the mafia finding her in Pennsylvania. Poca was still flawless, more beautiful than ever; she was every man's dream. Poca's mother started another family restaurant specializing in Spanish cuisine; they had the Spanish food game on lock. On the west coast it was mainly Mexicans—that's all you saw were Mexicans in Southern California. So when they came with fried bananas and stuffed potato balls fresh from the island, they made a killing. Poca's brothers worked at the restaurant, running it as the head managers.

The money they made was good, but they still didn't like California very much. Being Puerto Rican, it was harder for them to adjust around so many Mexicans. They didn't have any family on the west coast—they were out there on a no man's mission. Everything was different: the gangs, the way people dressed, the way the game was played. Poca's brothers were growing up and becoming young men. With their father's strength and brains embedded in their bloodline, they wanted their life in Puerto Rico back. They weren't interested in the California women at all and they didn't get along too well with the gangs either.

They were living in an immigrant community with Hondurans, El Salvadorians, and Mexicans. Every wall had graffiti of gangs marking their territories. There were rest in peace paintings of fallen soldiers with candles and flowers in front of the walls. The fastest growing gang was the MS 13 that originated in LA. It was an ongoing war in Cali, and they were the biggest reason behind it.

When Poca would get bored, she would turn on the television in an attempt to fall asleep. She'd flick through the channels until she found something to watch. She didn't watch reality shows, movies, or the sports channel. With all of the violence in California, the news was the only interesting thing. The MS 13s were being televised all over the news on a daily basis. They slayed thirty-two of their rival gang members with gory tactics like decapitating their arms, legs, fingers and toes.

Poca was freaked out thinking, *the motherfuckers are crazy.* Poca feared for her brothers and prayed that one day the Cali life wouldn't be their demise. They felt as though they could do or wear whatever they wanted, thinking they were invincible. Poca knew there were codes and rules, and if one disobeyed, they would pay for it with their life.

One day, Poca and her younger brother, Felix, were walking to the store to grab some top papers because they didn't have Dutch Masters there. Poca was more concerned of the MS 13s than any other gang, because Mexicans and Puerto Ricans hated each other. Whenever they would go anywhere, the Mexican girls would look at her as if she was fucking their baby fathers.

They continued walking toward the store, the streets crowded and packed with Mexicans. Poca and her brother were walking past a group of Mexicans who were all tatted with MS signs, no shirts, and black lochs, looking like they just committed homicide. They stared with stone faces, and all of them prepared to take any order given. At least nine males and three females started following Poca and her brother. Poca and her brother quickly realized they were being followed, having a sixth sense that something was about to happen.

"What's the problem? Are y'all following us?" Poca asked.

"What ESE you must have a pair of kahunas, home, this is MS turf. What set y'all claiming? What you representing, Crip, ESE?" the gang member said, throwing up his set.

"We don't gang bang. This is my little brother. We are from Puerto Rico. Do we look like gang members?" Poca said.

"That is disrespecting our turf, coming through our valley without permission. ESE. And we don't like you fucking spics anyway."

"Hey, papi, watch it Man who you calling a spic? We aren't trying to disrespect no one, but we not afraid of no-motherfucking-body," her brother said.

Poca pulled her brother back, using her arm to shield him. They were outnumbered and she really didn't want any problems. All they wanted was to go to the store and get what they needed. One of The MS members was offended and started pulling out a silver

.45 caliber. It was chrome with a pearl handle, infrared beam, with the extended clip hanging out of the bottom. He held it firmly in preparation to open fire. In California, it was shoot first then ask questions later. Everybody was about that gangster shit, even the bitches. One of the female gang members knew things were about to get real bloody, and could tell that Poca and her brother were new to the area and weren't banging.

"Come on, ESE, they not even from here, "carnal", they don't know any better. Give them a pass. Plus he cute and I like his heart," the girl banger said.

The MS member stared at Poca's brother, looking him up and down. The look on his face displayed anger, rage, as if he was looking forward to using his weapon. He had tattoos all over his face and skull with tear drops under both of his eyes. He put his gun back on his waist, making sure it was tucked properly and walked away. They turned around peacefully and went about their business.

The girl who saved them turned around and smiled. She had never seen a Puerto Rican in real life. Poca's brother smiled back as she walked away. Poca always tripped off her baby brother. He was hilarious, always getting attention from women. Both of her brothers reminded her of David, both having the personality and character he possessed. Felix was charming like David and Danny had David's temperament.

Poca missed everything about David: his looks, his dick, his swag, and, most of all, the way he talked to her. Poca anticipated the arrival of David any day now. She was the only person sending him letters and putting money on his books. Her thoughts were on David, where he was, how he was doing, did he move on and find a special love?

Poca was in need of some woman time away from her brothers. She left her place in a good mood, rolling up a blunt while driving her car. She drove down Firestone Boulevard, on her way to the liquor store to get a couple bottles, one brown and one clear. Poca loved music and always listened to the radio; it was always uplifting to her spirit. She continued down the street looking good, feeling good, and bopping her head to the tune of "Anaconda" by Nicki Manaj.

As she was driving, a truck on the side of her swerved and almost hit her. She saw it coming and swerved out of the way. She was almost finished rolling up her blunt when she was forced to swerve into the next lane. She tried to move back over, but she had already swiped the side of a green Neon low kit Lexus coupe. The windows were dark tint like Stevie Wonders' glasses; all she could see was a shadow inside the vehicle. The blunt flew into the air, spilling over her lap and floor.

"Fuck. Fuck," Poca said. She didn't want to stop in the middle of the street, knowing for sure that the police would come. So she put her turn signal on and turned inside of the plaza. The car followed her as Poca parked and got out of the car. The neon green Lexus had styling suicide doors, neon green lights on the door trims, and the rims were sparkling so clean that she could see her reflection. Under the rims there were neon green plates, and on the hood there was a mermaid dragon.

Poca knew this had to be a female's car, especially one with money. Poca was feeling the car crazy, and felt bad she scratched and dented the side of it. The girl got out of the car with a pen and paper. As she got out of the car, Poca watched as she walked with such confidence. The girl was beautiful, so beautiful that even Poca had to give her some props: she was one bad bitch. Her hair, platinum blonde at the roots with neon green tips, was cut short in an asymmetrical hair style. She wore neon green eye shadow, with neon green lip gloss. Poca couldn't resist, couldn't help but stare, not believing that a woman so perfect existed. She was petite with a nice stomach, slim waist, and her ass was perfectly round. She stood at 5 '3" with a tattoo of Ariel, The Little Mermaid, on the side of her upper thigh. She wasn't real thick, but thick enough, and every part of her body curved perfectly. The thing that's crazy was she was Asian. Never in a lifetime would Poca ever think an Asian girl could be this electrifying.

"I am so sorry. I did not mean to hit your car, but I do have full Insurance coverage. Please take my information. I know it was my fault, so, Mama, you don't have to call the police, okay?" Poca said.

The Asian girl looked Poca up and down, analyzing her appearance. She walked to the other side of her car and checked the damage. All she noticed was a small scrape and dent on the side of her door. The Asian girl was cool, being in a good mood.

"Cops? Me no call cops." She was in her car smoking Cali haze and didn't want to get in trouble either. Poca knew she had to be smoking some good shit, because the aroma was stinky, like a skunk had just walked passed.

"It's okay, my car's fine. My uncle runs the biggest body and paint shop here in southern California," the Asian said.

"Are you sure? I really want to take care of it. I was rolling up a Blunt and some asshole swerved into me," Poca said.

"You're Puerto Rican, aren't you? You never see no Spanish girl on the west coast, you must have just moved here," the Asian said.

"Yea,h and I be so bored I'm ready to just kill myself. Can't party and haven't had any dick in years," Poca said with a laugh.

"Girl, you serious. Sounds like you're being tortured. I can't believe I met a Puerto Rican on the West Coast. I have to show you around, show you off, California is going to love you! They call me, Achuri. Look, I'm a give you my number. Give me a call. I need someone to come to this party with me. So if you up to it, call me around nine and I will come pick you up in the limo. Wear something classy like a pretty dress and some stilettos. I want to see you looking extravagant tonight," the Asian said with lusty eyes.

The Asian walked away, blowing a kiss to Poca as she got inside of her Lexus and pulled off. Poca watched her as she walked away. She started cheesing from ear to ear, happy she'd met someone connected out in Cali.

Poca got in her car and pulled off. She went straight home and got dressed. Poca wasn't stupid—

she knew the girl liked her and that the girl probably liked girls. Poca never talked to a girl on a sexual level before, thinking, *I'm a just be cool with her till David get home*!

CHAPTER 22

COLD GAME

Murder witness

P oca was relaxing with candles lit and rose petals floating inside of her bath water. She took romantic, sensual baths and showers daily. She shaved her vagina, legs, and under arms, wishing a man was there to finish the job. She felt wonderful after her extravaganza with Achuri.

Poca was watching TV, smoking a blunt, and sipping on a chilled glass of red wine. She was concerned with the latest news of her family. She waited patiently, praying God was protecting them and keeping them out of harm's way.

Poca's phone rang. It was her brother, Danny. She anxiously answered the phone. "Brother, thank

1

God you're okay. I was fucking worried. Why hasn't anyone called me?" Poca said.

"Poca, we been spotted. Go lay low until I get there. I'm in Chicago on a layover. I will be home in a couple hours," Danny said, hanging up the phone.

Poca scrunched up her face with frustration, thinking, *what the fuck? How could they have found us?* Poca laid her phone down and continued smoking her perfectly rolled blunt. She plucked the ashes into the ashtray, still thinking and wondering what the hell was going on. She was tired of hiding, and figured if was going to happen, then it may as well finish now.

She grabbed her licensed gun and got dressed, waiting for her brother to arrive at the airport. Danny texted her to let her know he was at the airport. She left her apartment immediately, anxious to see what was going on. As she drove through traffic, she was amused and entertained with the life style of California. When she first moved to the West Coast, she hated everything about it. Now she admired and respected the gang codes, their mentality, culture, and the way they hustled.

She was stopped at a red light minding her own business, looking in the mirror to fix her lip gloss, when a vehicle pulled up. It was a navy blue old school Chevy, the paint was candy and the interior decorated with navy blue C's on the cocaine white upholstery. The car started hopping on three wheels. She smiled and was pleased to see it.

The light changed and the car pulled up to the next light. Poca looked in her mirror, noticing a red car speeding up. The red car stopped on the side of the blue car. All of the doors opened and four men wearing all red got out. They all had big automatic weapons.

"What the fuck?" Poca asked.

The blue car tried to pull off, but the people in red opened fire, spraying a rapid amount of bullets within seconds. The guy slumped over on the wheel of his grain. They all ran over to the car and started emptying their clips. His body shook viciously like Denzel's body on the movie *Training Day*. One of the killers ran over to Poca's car and wrote down her license plate. He took a picture with a camera phone and then hopped back into the car and pulled off.

Poca was clueless, not knowing what to do. All she knew was that it was none of her business. She pulled off with her heart beating hard and ears hurting. She was shocked at what had just occurred and thought, *what the fuck, this shit crazy out here*.

CHAPTER 23

FREE  MAN

A living legend

The big day was finally here! After two hard, lonely, stressful years David was ready to pack his bags, never even telling his celly that he was leaving until the day before his departure. He started packing all of his belongings in a brown box. His celly already knew what time it was. Anytime an inmate packed their bags they're on their way out of the door.

"Stay up, dog, remember love life, live long, and be free, my G."

David nodded, dapped his celly up, and walked out of the cell holding his box. Everyone watched with envy wishing it was them getting ready to go home to their family. He strolled with a pimp lean. As he continued walking through the long hall of the prison, he saw a face he could never forget. The Philly guy he had the confrontation with in the yard mopped and swept the halls. He had a scar on the side of his face shaped like Florida. They locked eyes, both of them not blinking, not smiling, neither one of them willing to back down. The Philly guy dropped the mop onto the floor as if he was going to retaliate. The C.O. saw what was getting ready to occur and quickly stopped it. He sped David up the hall, escorting him out of the prison gates.

David walked with his box and a small bag over his shoulder, dressed in all black and he wearing black sunglasses; looking like a silverback gorilla. He took his glasses off, staring into the air and smelling the aroma of freedom. He started walking toward the bus stop to wait for the city bus. *I hope this bus don't take too fucking long. I'm not trying to miss this flight.* David sat on the bench, listening to his CD player. He was America's nightmare: too deadly, too monstrous to be a free man with no charges and only a month of parole to walk off. Poca sent David an airplane ticket and money to catch the bus to the airport. He walked out of the jail with his head high, his chin up, and with the wind behind his back.

He was glowing, looking like a young prince. His hair was thick and long, braided in corn rows with a sharp line up. His chest sat out, his arms were humungous, and his back was like a cobra's head. David was in top shape and his thoughts were clear, even though they were hardened. He went to jail at a hundred and sixty pounds and left jail at two-hundred and sixteen pounds, all solid with no body fat.

David got onto the bus heading toward the airport. He was happy to be free, happy he could live life, happy that he could kill King and take his daughter back. The whole ride to the airport he thought about revenge on the man who kidnapped his daughter.

David had never been on an airplane, so he was nervous, but at the same time not caring. He got onto the airplane and, looking around, put his box and bag on top of the overhead and buckled up. The plane took off and he fell asleep, and then David woke up to the sunny sight of California. As they were landing, he stared at his new beginning. David had never in his life seen a palm tree, never seen a car on three wheel motion. He understood the gang trade, the color code; he was ready and looking forward to robbing southern California blind.

The birds were beautiful, much different than the birds that soared on the east coast. David got off of the plane with everything that he owned in one box and a small bag. He still was dressed in his state prison clothes. He was starting over, seeking a new beginning, with no money, no jewelry, absolutely nothing. He figured Poca would already be doing something, either gambling or hustling. David had it in his mind that he was going to rob everything moving. He knew the first thing he had to do was get his hands on a pistol. In his mind he was invincible, indestructible, and if your body pumped blood, you couldn't stop him.

David sat in front of the airport smoking a Newport cigarette, waiting patiently for his Queen to arrive. He missed her and hadn't seen her in years.

A car pulled up to the curb, honking and blasting music. She parked the car and got out with such confidence, such structure, walking as if she was stomping a runway. She was smiling ear to ear, happy to see the man she loved. Her hair was curly, wet, jet black, and her skin was slightly darker with a tone of caramel. Poca knew David's attractions; he liked a woman in tights, fitted dresses, and stilettos. She decided to wear his favorite colors of purple and turquoise like the Charlotte Hornets. She'd already had an outfit and accessories specifically for this day. All white tights with a purple and turquoise thong, showing just a little. Her shirt was purple and turquoise tied behind her back, showing her new tattoo. Poca was flawless, impeccable, still bowlegged and walking like the ground belonged to her!

She was thicker, having gained seven pounds since the last time David had seen her. When he realized that it was her, he stood up and took off his black glasses with a facial expression that spoke of lust and affection. Laying his bag and box down on the wooden chair, he walked to Poca.

She watched, looking him up and down, mesmerized by his new muscular body. They both opened their arms, smiling from cheek to cheek. They ran to each other and David caught her in midair. He lifted her up over his head, showing her his new man power. Poca screamed in joy, not wanting to be put down. He slowly lowered her as she wrapped her legs around his waist.

"Papi, I missed you so much."

David had her by the ass, using one palm for each butt cheek. He let her down while kissing her gently on the lips. They started horse playing in the parking lot, ending in each other's arms and lip locked in a heat of passion. David threw his hands up like he was ready to slap box. They had that type of relationship: play fighting, wrestling, and then making erotic magic.

"Damn, baby, you have to be God's best creation. Look at you all grown up now. You're a red carpet event. My life hasn't been the same since you left!" David said.

Poca blushed and smiled. She always admired the way David talked to her. She liked to be charmed, a man with a sense of humor, and most of all she liked a man strong enough to handle her feistiness.

"I didn't want to leave, but there was a certain lifestyle that my family was involved in, so we had no choice but to run. I promise to tell you everything. Papi, I have to introduce you to my brother. Y'all are so much alike and he can't wait to meet you."

Poca helped David carry his things to the car, then they both got inside and pulled off. The only thing on David's mind was sex and Poca was thinking the same thing. He needed some pussy bad. His hand had become his girlfriend in prison. All he could think of was sticking his tongue in some pussy. He was still the same, not losing one pep in his step, but being more advanced, charming, and handsome. He was now twenty-one years old. His intelligence level raised dramatically and his word play was broader. The knowledge that he received about his condition wasn't enough to change his thoughts of dying. In his mind, death was waiting around the corner and so was the devil.

They needed a few items to get their evening started off right. They purchased a few things, including juice, chips, blunts, and sugar. David grabbed a box of condoms thinking, *fuck that, I'm not giving HIV to Poca!* They got what they needed from the store and walked out holding hands. They got into the car, pulling off, and headed straight to Poca's apartment. As they were pulling up, Poca noticed something was different. There was the same red car that shot up the blue old school car at the traffic light. Poca thought, *what the fuck? How ironic.* So Poca pulled up to her parking spot, grabbed her gun from her purse and took the safety off.

David sat there not understanding what was going on. "What's up, mami, you good?" David said.

"I don't know, Papi, but a while ago I witnessed that same car open fire on a man, killing him. Babe, it was like a movie scene. They pulled up on the side of this blue car and started shooting on some Wild West shit," Poca said.

David thought about it. *This isn't a coincidence. They're on her top!* David told Poca to give him the gun. He grabbed it and put it on his waist. He told Poca to stay in the car. He got out looking like a real OG out of state prison. Wearing a white tank top with some tan dickeys on, David stood at the back of Poca's car, took off his loch's, and watched the car as it pulled off.

Poca got out of the car and grabbed David's hand, walking him into her apartment. She'd left her cell phone at home, now realizing she had four missed calls and two text messages from Achuri, the Asian girl from the car accident incident. As she was reading the text messages, David walked up behind her, enjoying the beauty of her perfectly round ass. He wrapped his muscular arms around her gently, smelling her hair, laying his face on the side of her shoulder. He held her from behind, letting her feel the massiveness of his erect penis, grinding it side to side on her ass. He moved her curly hair to the side and started sucking on the soft skin of her neck. Her body trembled as her vagina released moisture, moisturizing her purple and turquoise panties. David hadn't felt a woman's warmth in years and Poca hadn't felt a man, so the energy was intense.

She dropped her phone on the carpet floor, forgetting that it was in the palm of her hand. Her eyes closed as she remembered the last time they made love. She turned around with a facial expression that said *fuck me now*. Poca started French kissing David and massaging his penis through his pants. She wanted his dick in her mouth badly, thinking, *I am going to suck the skin off this man*. Poca's vagina was extra tight; it was itching and needed David to scratch it. She wanted him to fuck her good, releasing all her fantasies and imaginations out on her body. Poca started unbuckling his belt with her mouth, watching his pants fall to the floor. She pulled down his boxers and started massaging his penis with both of her hands. Poca loved sucking dick; it was her motivator, loving the way a man would react when she did her little tricks.

"Damn, Papi, you still can't take it? All that dick and you can't take my little tongue."

"Mami, you know that's my weakness, that tongue's ferocious. I'm not even going to lie to you," David said.

David was scooting and crawling back begging for mercy as she worked her hands on the tip of his penis. Poca was nice with it, she did it nice and gentle, not scraping it with her teeth at all. David made her stop because he didn't want to explode. He pushed her head away and stood up, needing to feel the inside of her.

Poca already knew what to do, knew what he liked. She told him to smack her ass and pull her hair. She started playing with her pussy, moaning in Spanish. David couldn't wait to taste her, he loved eating pussy and especially from the back. David thought pussy juice was nutritious and had vitamins, thinking *anything that can create life has to be full of vitamins and minerals*. The blood through David's penis vessels filled up fast. He was so hard that it hurt. He needed to fuck badly. *Imagine being locked up in prison for a year and a half, no pussy, no woman!*

He started kissing her vagina, enjoying every bit of it. Her vagina lips were soft, plump, brownish pink

203

with no smell. David started sucking on her clitoris, trying to fuck her with his tongue. His oral game was magnificent and twice as nice since the last time he ate her vagina. Poca was amazed, honored, as the warmth of his tongue melted her. He was strategic at everything he did, knowing the perfect time to strike. So when he ate pussy it was a buildup, when the body became closer to climax his finger would be his murder weapon. He stuck his index finger inside of her vagina, going directly to her roof spot. He started using his finger as if he was telling her to come here, while flicking her clitoris with the tip of his tongue at the same time.

Poca started screaming, her moans erotic and pleasurable. Poca squeezed David's head with her hands as she became a volcano releasing warm lava onto his face. He smiled, laughing, and knowing he was one of the best pussy eaters that God had ever created.

David grabbed his box of condoms out of his pocket. He ripped it open and was getting ready to put one on. Poca looked up and said, "Papi, I need to feel your skin. I'm on the shot, babe, don't worry."

David was tempted, but couldn't comply with her request since he'd already had it in his heart to spare Poca's life. David respected Poca most of all, he loved her and didn't want to lose her like he lost Danielle. David thought of something to say quickly. "Baby, I haven't had no pussy in two years, I need to enjoy this moment."

So David put the condom on. He couldn't wait to feel her oven juice box. David turned Poca around, laying her on her back. Her body was perfect, glowing, you could see the light glistening off of her Spanish body. David climbed in between her legs and pushed himself inside of her. The feeling was breathtaking.

He stroked her gently, not wanting to rush at all. "Don't rush, baby, this loving not going nowhere. Slow it down."

David pushed himself inside of her further and further. Every time he inched in, she would scoot back, running from the size of his anaconda penis. He held her tighter sitting still, not moving, and sucked her bottom lip. He wanted her body to relax, adjust; she bit his shoulder, trying to take the pleasurable pain. David could feel her loosening, stretching, and he now knew she was ready to be fucked. Poca was slippery, allowing his penis to slide in and out of her easily. He talked to her nasty like a slutty whore; she loved to be talked to that way.

"Yea, you gone take this dick, mami, give me that pussy right now. You love this black Mandingo, don't you? Yeah, I know. Yeah, I know I was in jail dreaming about this pussy!" David grunted.

David tried to keep his poise and control, but not having any sex in two years made it difficult to withstand. Poca was enjoying every moment, staring at David with desire and fire in her eyes. He put both of his hands under her ass, cuffing each of her butt cheeks. Poca could hardly take it as he started fucking her deeper and deeper. David was trying his hardest not to cum, but every time he went in he would get closer to a nut.

"Damn, girl, this one is going to be big, fuck, uh, uh, uh, oh shit...Ahh hhh..."David's body shook uncontrollably. "You Puerto Rican animal. I love your ass, uhhhh. Oh my god, that was crazy. I needed that!" David said.

They both laid there holding each other tightly as if they would never see each other again. The real Bonnie and Clyde were back together. David had his once hustle queen back in his arms again.

CHAPTER 24

POWER & GLORY

Avarice for finance

D avid sought a new beginning with no money, no jewelry, absolutely nothing. After sitting in prison thinking and strategizing, he devised a plan of revenge. He knew he wasn't strong enough to war with King, who was notorious and powerful; a man with money and power is never to be taken lightly. King would be patiently waiting to snatch David's heart from his chest with his bare hands. King hated David with a passion, having the upper hand as he raised Devunyae as if she was his. His Auntie was a hustler turned nurse and King was her favorite nephew. It was nothing for her to give David's daughter shots and checkups, so King wouldn't have to take her to a doctor's office.

David planned on staying in Cali until he got his cash up, and then head back to Pennsylvania A.S.A.P. There was no way he would be in California enjoying palm trees and sandy beaches while his enemy raised his daughter.

Poca had been through hell and back after all her losses and was ready to leave the west coast anyway. She had her own hustle going on and her mother left her with a substantial amount of money. Poca was willing and felt obligated to take care of David until he got back on his feet.

It was Friday morning and David was asleep, snoring and cuddled up in Poca's panda bear fur blanket. Poca was in the mood to cook and David hadn't had a home cooked meal in years. She wanted to surprise him with naked breakfast in bed. Some maple turkey sausage links, eggs over easy, grits, and Hungry Jack pancakes. She was naked, smoking a blunt, and cooking at the same time, something she did every morning. She loved opening up the blinds, turning on the music, lighting her incense as the sunlight blazed through the blinds. She hadn't seen or talked to Achuri since David had been there. Achuri had been texting, calling from blocked numbers, blowing Poca's phone up.

Poca started flipping the pancakes so they could brown on each side. She heard her Pomeranian, named Daisy, barking at the door. When the doorbell chimed, she took the pan off of the stove so the pancakes wouldn't burn. She walked to the door and looked out of the peep hole realizing it was Achuri. Poca was startled and couldn't believe she showed up at her doorstep. Achuri was the over protective type, and got jealous when a man or woman would lust after Poca.   She decided not to answer the door, not wanting her to see David.

She watched Achuri pull off, thinking, *Wow, no she didn't. Damn, if I don't answer, that means I'm busy, damn!* She went back to the kitchen to finish David's breakfast. Poca and Achuri had gotten kind of tight in the small time they knew each other. They went to a few house parties, clubs, casinos, and Poca met the rest of the Asian circle. Poca met her uncle, one of her brothers, and a couple of her cousins. Achuri wasn't into everything that her family was into. She would party, have fun, but for the most part she didn't have to hustle. Her family was knee deep in hustling, gambling, robbing and beefing with rivals. They was called "the Asian Gang." They had the biggest car detail and paint shop in southern California. She was amazed, impressed, and fascinated when Achuri took her to the car shop. It was crazy; Poca never met any Asians that were cool, fly, and gangsters at the same time. They were all in there smoking, popping pills, listening to Asian music, and having a good time. Poca knew they were getting mega money, she could smell it.

Achuri walked her to the back office where her uncle was at. She knew the rules that it wasn't allowed, nor tolerated, but she never paid her uncle any mind. Poca followed her into the office. There were two older Asian men, one with long, black thin hair and one with a bald head with a long ponytail.

Achuri's uncle stood up, yelling aggressively in their language. The two older men turned around and stared at Poca. They were putting money into three money counters, at least a hundred grand. When Poca glanced, she noticed a bucket full of ecstasy pills. She thought, *Yea they're slanging major pills out of here.*

Achuri grabbed her by the arm and they both stormed out of the office and left the Detail shop. The whole time she was dropping Poca off, Poca's mind was spinning. She'd never seen that much money, ecstasy pills, and Asian bosses in real life. Poca thought, *My mom left me two-hundred grand, I'm about to turn the fuck up!*

Nevertheless, David woke up to breakfast in bed feeling good to have a beautiful woman cater to him. He watched her walk to him, naked and bringing him a plate of food. The smell filled the air, and her body was looking like it belonged on the plate itself. David's stomach started craving the tastes of the food his queen prepared. He still was on prison time, stuffing everything in his mouth in five minutes. He devoured the food, leaving nothing on the plate, nothing!

David got out of bed and took his finished dishes to the kitchen. He was walking in his boxers, making Poca drool as his dick bounced side to side. She stared at his six pack and newly shaped body and how perfectly he was put together. She couldn't resist it, it was looking too delicious as she walked toward him. She was still horny, love thirsty, and after she fucked David she realized the lesbian route wasn't for her.

Poca sat David down on the couch and started giving him head. The taste of his black skin was erotic to her, and it always made her extra horny. Her pussy was getting wetter by the second, dripping down the side of her legs. David was caught up in the moment, still holding his composure, stopping her to get a condom. Poca hated condoms—she didn't like the feel of them and got kind of turned off by the thought of it. David already had it drilled in his head to never hurt a woman he loved again. Poca was getting a weird feeling, wondering why David didn't want to have unprotected sex with her.

As a million memories rushed through her head at one time, Poca started thinking, *This isn't like papi. Something is wrong!*

Poca just went with the flow, getting on top of him and riding him. Her thoughts immediately vanished as she sat on his massive penis. David kissed her breasts, sucking her hardened nipples and enjoying the wonderful view. He remembered when they were younger, how she would squirt whenever he sucked her titties. After they finished, Poca got off of the couch, almost stumbling, and walked to the bathroom. She opened the door and closed it, staring into the mirror at her beautiful face. She kept wondering why David didn't want to fuck her raw. She was confused, but more worried than anything.

CHAPTER 25

DARK ROAD

No chill button

Life on the west coast was different for David. The palm trees, the houses, the weather, and mainly the three wheel motion on the candy painted cars. It was weird seeing that Mexicans outnumbered the blacks five to one. David didn't know that most of California used to be Mexico. And the Mexicans in California Arizona, etc. are mostly 3rd 5th generation Americans, On the east coast you'd barely see a Mexican and, if so, they stayed out of the way. David had no fears, no chill button. Why be scared when he awaited death anyway? He didn't have time for any remorse—at the end of the day, blood was the only outcome. First he had to come up and get his mind right, money right, then he'd be ready for war. The only person David had in his corner was Poca—he hadn't met her older brother yet. HE wasn't too concerned about getting fresh, thinking *Fuck clothes, fuck sneakers, and fuck jewelry. All I need is a come up and some cash in my hands, so I can show this nicca I'm ready.*

David used to try and escape the thoughts, the nightmares, the souls that waited for him at the cross roads. He knew his life was a war zone, and his only purpose was to die a soldier's death. In the mind of a troubled boy, the stories they showed on television were of false hopes and false advertisements. There wasn't any peace, any happiness, and no pot of gold at the end of the rainbow. It was bullshit, asinine; the message was like bait hoping a stupid fish would bite. David was clear on who he was now, no longer having pity on himself. He fully understood his destiny, even though he once yearned for a loving family and for someone to genuinely love him. He understood his life would end lonely and there would be no one at the funeral mourning him. While David was in prison, he went to church every Sunday reading, studying, and learning more about God. His relationship with the Lord now was all he needed. Even though David disagreed with the cards he was dealt, through the trials and tribulations he endured, he still grew to believe in his higher power. David was scheming and plotting, watching everything that moved. He knew Poca was used to living a certain lifestyle; always on a higher echelon.

Poca was asleep, exhausted, trying to get used to all of this dick in her life now. She was in deep slumber with a light snore, perfectly tucked in her blanket. Poca's phone started ringing. David paid it no mind until the calls continued. He looked at the phone and it said "boo." He scrunched his face, thinking, *Oh yeah.* David answered without saying a word and, once he heard a female's voice, he hung up.

He went through her phone, reading all of her messages. He saw that she had a secret: a new life and a special friend on the low. David didn't care, he was just being nosey, just fishing around seeing if he could catch a fish. When he saw the Asian girl was sending pictures of a shaved vagina, sucking dildos, and talking about how Poca's pussy tasted, he laughed. He never would've thought she was into girls.

David stayed on point, thinking three steps ahead like chess moves. When he saw all of the pictures of them at the club, looking like money, it caught his attention. Achuri's car, jewelry, Gucci this, Hermes that, the aroma of money was all through the air. He knew Poca; she would never fuck with a bitch unless she was bossy like her.

David never said anything about his snooping to her and, instead, waited patiently and watched for clues. Poca started selling ecstasy pills at the restaurant, grossing a substantial amount of money. Her phone popped crazy, clients buying ten to twenty pills at a time. She had an endless supply since Achuri's family was supplying the whole city with pills. Any pill you wanted, they could get their hands on it: pain pills, mollies, perks, ecstasy, so it was nothing for Poca to get her hands on them.

So one day her phone started ringing and someone from Eastside LA wanted some pills. Poca had just sold fifteen pills and didn't have enough for the order. David figured Archuri had to be supplying her. David put two and two together and Poca was being very secretive because she knew his mentality.

"Mami, what's happening? I got a few things I need to talk to you about," David said.

"What, papi?"

"Well, you know you've been gone a long time and a lot has changed since you left baby. My knees are a lot deeper, you feel me? I'm in a war that I have to finish; my hands are bloody much more than before. I have powerful people that want me dead, my head on a platter. I have a daughter now, Poca, and the person I'm warring with kidnapped her. So once I get my money right, I'm going back to PA and killing that motherfucker and taking my daughter back. You feel me?" David said.

Poca sat there in silence, listening with a face full of questions. She figured some things would have changed, but never this. She knew she was the one who left him, so whatever his new life was she would have to except it.

"So how are you planning to get your money, Papi? This life over here is different from the east coast. They have codes, you just can't sell drugs here, and they'll kill you quickly as day. It's too dangerous, baby."

"Nah, I'm not trying to sell no drugs. I am going to rob a few people and go back to PA. Then we are going to move to Miami and live our lives like Kings and Queens. I am at war, Poca..."

Before David could say anything else, gun fire sounded. David told Poca to get down, as the bullets tore through the house. It was like the fourth of July, automatic weapons spraying, letting off rapid rounds. Bullets came through windows, the wall. Poca screamed as bullets ricocheted through her house. David took cover, looking out of the window seeing the same car from before. The car pulled off and headed down the street.

David ran over to Poca. "Mami, you good?"

Running to her purse for her gun, she opened the door and ran outside of the house. Poca was vexed, wishing she could retaliate. Her house was Swiss cheese, looking like the cartoon character Sponge Bob. All of the neighbors stared outside of their widows, watching what was going on from a distance. In California, everyone minded their own business and no one called the police, ever. David and Poca walked back into the house. She was pissed and crying; she needed to vent. Since her losses, Poca had been popping more pills and smoking more blunts in an attempt to not think of her loved ones. The California life was suddenly getting to her: all of the violence, the gangs, and mainly the Mexicans.

"Papi, I have things I have to tell you. I can't take it anymore. I know that I smile and grin like everything in my life is perfect, but I'm done trying to seem happy. The reason I left PA is because my father was in the Spanish mafia, and when he tried to get out they killed him. Then they put a hit out on me and my family, so we left Puerto Rico and came to PA. When they found out where we were, we had no choice but to flee or die! So after running and hiding, my mother and brothers got tired of it and went back to Puerto Rico to cut the head of the snake," Poca said.

"So what happened, Mami?"

Poca started crying as her mind wandered off to a dark road. She had skeletons in her closet that she'd been dealing with for years. Poca was tired of it all and sometimes felt as if she was ready to be with her father in heaven.

"To make a long story short, they cut the head of the snake. The war is finally over." Poca started rolling up a blunt. "I'm getting the fuck out of California."

David knew those gang bangers would continue terrorize Poca until she either moved or they killed her. He figured now was the perfect time to let her know of his plans. David and Poca went over to her mother's restaurant. She finally introduced David to her brother, Danny. She couldn't keep anything from her brother; he could read straight through her. He knew something was bothering her.

"Sis, what happened?"

"Danny, oh my God, I seen these gangbangers murder someone. They came and took a picture of me and wrote down my license plate. After I picked David up from the airport, they were parked out front of my house. Earlier today they came and shot up my crib. It's bullet holes all through that motherfucker!"

Poca's brother was livid, irate. He hated for anyone to hurt his family. Poca began to second guess David and her brother meeting. She knew they were both savages. They both had very short tempers, big egos, and didn't give a fuck. They would eventually click, becoming one, and cause the world extreme devastation. They would rob everything from banks, houses, meat trucks—whatever they could.

They were all sitting down at the table eating sweet fried bananas, Spanish rice, and meatballs. The day was beautiful, with a sun full of rays that lit up the sky as sunset approached. Everyone was outside enjoying the weather, the car washes were all packed. People were cleaning their rims, vacuuming out their cars, and letting their systems blast. Everyone was getting ready for the big concert at the arena tonight. All of the main radio stations broadcasted about this concert all day. It was E-40, Too Short, Keisha Cole, and Ice Cube. When David heard them say they were featuring Post Up "Early Bird Mob," he got hype.

"Oh shit, my boy, them is my dawgs. Damn, they popping out here? That's crazy, my boys did it. I'm going to that concert. Watch how they react when they see your boy," David said.

"Oh, they from Harrisburg, Papi? I like that song "Never Know" that be playing on the radio. They

always on the radio out here. I'm with it, let's go!"
Poca said.

CHAPTER 26

NEVER SLEEP

Wolf Pack

Poca wasn't in the mood to dress casual or dressy. The temperature was in the mid 90's, which meant the arena would be hella hot, humid, and she would sweat out her attire anyway. She loved wearing her hair wet and curly and it always turned David on. She did her hair and makeup, wearing pink lip gloss with a sprinkle of pink shadow. She put on her pink tights with a white and pink Gucci shirt.

Everyone dressed, Poca and David left the house on their way to pick up her brother Danny. They pulled up fifteen minutes later honking the horn.

Poca's brother poked his head out of the door and told them to park and give him a second.

"Damn, Papi. He always does this. He can never be ready," Poca said.

"He coming, babe, chill out. You funny, Mami, over there looking like heaven itself," David said.

Poca's brother came out with a big bottle of Spanish Rum. He lifted it in the air, smiling while lifting up his shirt to show a giant, 50 cal handgun.

"Damn, Papi, why you always have to bring a gun? We're going to a concert not a shootout, brother. See, that's why I don't like going places with him because he starts acting crazy and shit. Ugh." Poca just had to shake her head and laugh.

On their way to the concert, Poca wanted to stop and get some blunts. She hated being sober and wanted to get high before they went inside the concert. You never know if security gone be tripping about the weed smoke. They stopped at the gas station and pulled up to one of the pumps. Poca asked David and her brother if they wanted anything, but they both declined. Getting out of the car, she walked inside of the store and got what she needed. As she was at the counter, she noticed the same red car with one guy pumping the gas and the other just sitting on the passenger side. Poca's heart started pacing as she hurriedly exited the store to tell her brother and David.

"David, that's the same red car that shot my house up. It's only two of them. I should go shoot them motherfuckers," Poca said.

"What? Sis, chill out. I got this. Where they at, sis? I was praying that we ran into them."

Poca's brother told her to pull over at the Chick-fil-A across the street. He already had his weapon ready, locked, and loaded. Danny couldn't wait to take his fury out on someone. His nights were restless. Every time he fell asleep, his father would reappear in his dreams. He looked for any reason to get into a beef with anybody, anywhere—it didn't matter, and that's why Poca didn't want him and David to get together.

David and Danny both got out of the car and Poca drove across the street to wait as instructed. David didn't have a gun yet, so Poca's brother took the lead. They walked over to the red car and the one guy was still pumping gas.

David told Danny, "I'm-a snatch the driver and you get the passenger." They walked over to them.

"Wassup, bra," one of the men spoke.

"Wassup, bra. What you know about that B word?" David said.

"I'm blood, nicca, all day. Brim gang and then he started throwing up his set."

David quickly snatched the driver up by the neck, like a lion grabbing a baby elk. When he grabbed him, his whole body shook and the gas pump came out of the car. Poca's brother pulled out his 50 Cal, cocking it back, pointing it to the passenger's head. They were both lunching, slipping, not being aware of their surroundings.

"You shot my sister's house up. Tell me why I shouldn't pull this trigger and take your life, punto?" Poca brother said.

"Your sister? I don't know your sister, bra," the passenger said

"Oh, so now you got jokes. You acting like you stupid now, right, fuck boy," Poca's brother said.

The guy saw Poca's brother getting angrier by the second. He tried to sneak and reach for the gun was tucked beneath the car seat. Poca's brother was on point and dug the gun into his temple, ready to squeeze the trigger. Once David saw him biting his lip and looking side to side, he knew he was going to blast. David figured they had cameras in the gas station and he wasn't wearing a mask. So in his mind he was praying that he didn't pull the trigger.

Poca's brother dug the gun deeper into the side of the man's temple. "I wish you would, motherfucker. Give me that Goddamn pistol. Give it here or eat this slug." The guy gave Danny the gun in submission, and he took then handed it to David.

"Now, I'm-a tell you niccaz this one time, and one time only: leave my sister alone. She has nothing to do with y'all bullshit. We are from Puerto Rico, and rats die with their tongues in their kid's mouths. Don't fuck with my family again. Forget about us and we forget about you. I know your faces now. My sister not a rat and would die before she snitched," Danny said.

David and Danny both walked away, pointing their guns at the gang members as they crossed the street to the Chick-fil-A. They both got in the car and pulled off. As they headed toward the concert, Poca looked at her brother and David, waiting for someone to say what happened. They both sat there in silence.

David was shocked and surprised by the way her brother handled the situation. He had no idea he was a soldier, a gangster, an honorable man like him. If David fucked with Poca's brother the long way, he was certain he would come to PA and fight this war with him. Poca watched as David tucked his new gun. She already knew that was all he wanted since he'd been home. There would be no stopping him now.

David was back.

CHAPTER 27

THE FIGHT

To fight for

David, for once, was enjoying life for the first time since he'd been out of prison. He had a woman on his side who had her finances in order. She looked out for him, helping him make it through the trial of being released from jail and having nothing. David often thought of Danielle and the mistakes he made that led to her demise. As much as he regretted what happened to his first love, he knew he had to move on. He was cold in nature, so it didn't take long for him to forget about Danielle. His only focus was to find his baby girl Devunyae and start a new life with Poca.

The ride home was rather silent as David schemed in his mind who his first target should be.

1

Poca knew David was a stick up kid, having pulled licks together in the past. As Poca and Achuri slowly drifted apart, she felt the urge to tell David about her little journey. Poca may have looked beautiful on the outside, but the inside of her was dark. If you weren't on her team or a close member, she didn't give a damn about you. Poca had been facing adversity for years now and was finally coming to grips that this was her reality. Since David had been home, she started to forget all about Achuri. David had been fucking her every day, giving her that dick she always yearned for.

After the gas station incident, Poca wasn't really in the mood to be bothered with people. She told David that she didn't want to go to the concert. David understood. All she wanted to do was go home, pack up, and leave California. They turned back around and headed toward the house. As she pulled up, she noticed Achuri sitting in her drive way.

"Damn, bitch, where you been? I been blowing up your phone for days now. Like what type a shit you on?" Achuri yelled.

"What? I been busy taking care of things, mami. Why, what's going on?" Poca asked.

"You been acting real distant, real funny, and I see you have a new friend. Is that your body guard?" Achuri asked sarcastically.

Poca was already in a bad mood. Before Achuri could say anything, she slapped her across the face and grabbed her by the hair. They began to wrestle on the ground. Poca was on top with her knees holding down

Achuri's arms. She grabbed a wad of her hair as she jerked her head around, so she could face her.

"Listen, bitch. Don't you ever disrespect me or anyone I am around. You hear me? You taking this jealous shit way too far," Poca said

Poca let her hair go as her brother and David pulled them apart. Achuri walked away shocked, surprised, yet turned on even more. Achuri loved rough sex, and the message she got was of sexual lust and desire. She knew she would see Poca again, but her only problem was getting David out of the way.

Achuri got in her car and sped off. Poca and David stared at each other. Poca knew she had some explaining to do. David wasn't the least concerned with the relationship Poca started with Achuri. He laid his pipe down, knowing she wasn't any competition. His only concern was robbing Achuri, knowing she was a golden goose.

CHAPTER 28

ASIAN GANG

The ninja boys

David had his plan figured out, so all he had to do was convince Poca into letting him rob Achuri and the car shop. He had a gun now, and Danny was about that life—the real ride or die type. David could use him in the future, so he wanted to secure their relationship.

"*Mami, I already talked to your brother about it. Let's take their money, go get my daughter, and move to Miami. Fuck them. You said it yourself that you're ready to leave California,*" David said.

After a whole week of trying to talk Poca into the lick, he knew he was going to have to work a little harder. He decided to give her a special night, one she would remember for the rest of her life. It was Tuesday night and the air was dry and the moon shined on the earth. David was still protecting himself, not wanting to give Poca a death sentence. Poca never told him her darkest secret, and didn't plan on it. In her mind, she just wanted to be happy, have a family, and have someone to live her days out with.

They were coming back from the movies, both feeling good, having smoked two L's and popping an E pill before the movie. Poca turned David onto pills. He was now popping pills and smoking weed on a daily basis. David was hitting the blunt and reminiscing on the first time they smoked a wooley together. He smiled and continued hitting the blunt; he was finally back with his hustle queen.

After they finished smoking the blunt, David passed her the bottle. They both started drinking, getting drunk by the second. As Poca drove, David started playing with her pussy, putting his fingers up to his nose to smell them. He was rubbing his fingers in a circular motion around her clit through her tights. He stared in her eyes with fire, desire, knowing what made her pussy jump. Poca liked confidence, she liked for her man to show power and authority like a King. As David sucked on her shoulder, she pulled up to a red light. David quickly took her tights off at the red light, not caring if they were being watched.

The light turned green and they pulled off, David playing with her pussy again. Poca was so wet that she was staining her car seat.

"Oh shit I'm fucking my seats up," she noted, and laughed.

David ignored her and pulled her breast out of her shirt. Sucking them with his tongue, he thought to himself, *I'm about to beat this pussy down.* David pulled his pants down with his erect penis standing at attention. He rolled an XL magnum all the way down to the base.

Poca was breathing hard, shivering and waiting for her perfectly shaved pussy to be punished. She was tipsy and in the mood to be fucked, no loving. She wanted to be treated like a slut. She felt like screaming, and David was the perfect man for the job. The thought of his massiveness touching her spot was too much; the thought almost caused her to run the truck off of the road.

David made her pull off to the closest exit. She pulled over at a car wash and went inside the automatic washer. She put ten dollars in for two washes. David pushed the button for his seat to go all the way back. He was a lot bigger, so he realized it wasn't as easy to fuck in a car anymore. He grabbed Poca from across the driver's side and laid her back against the dash board. He licked his fingers, putting moisture on the condom. He knew that was getting ready to smash her; in his mind, he wasn't showing any remorse. He put her legs in the air, lifting them all the way back. Her pussy was beautiful sitting out perfectly. David pushed his manhood inside of her, her pussy talking, whispering as he entered inside. Stroking her with the long stroke, he touched her spot easily from this position. Poca was going crazy, screaming his name, telling him to fuck her harder. Every time he went the whole way inside, she would get closer to an orgasm. David was speeding up, pounding her, enjoying as she begged for more. The truck was rocking as it was almost finished getting cleaned. David turned Poca around, closing her legs as he fucked her from behind. David was gunning her, tearing her out of the frame, and he knew she was getting ready to splash. He was so far inside of her that he could feel her pussy pulsing. He knew she was a squirter, and every time she came from the back she would squirt.

"Oooh, Papi. Oh my God."

Moaning and screaming from pain and pleasure, she squirted all over David's shirt. David loved every bit of it. He let her finish squirting and then dived right back in. He was getting close to an orgasm, he felt it, and knew it was going to be a big one. As he was pumping her hard, he felt her pussy get wetter and, before he could think, he blasted.

David growled, roaring, as he climaxed. He laid on her for thirty seconds, still inside of her. As his penis softened, he pulled out. When he looked down to take the condom off, he realized it was ripped. His heart started beating faster, his whole mood changing. David would be devastated if he gave her HIV, too. He would be crushed.

Poca could feel something was wrong, remembering the signs and face he made when he was troubled. When she looked down, seeing that the condom broke, she started thinking. She wondered why David wouldn't fuck her raw—it had been months since his release and he still strapped up. When she first met him, she tried her hardest to get him to put a condom on. Now she couldn't get him to take it off!

"Papi, what's the matter? Is there something wrong?"

"Nah, everything cool, I'm straight. It's just, out of nowhere my daughter popped up in my mind," David said.

Poca was starting to put two and two together. Back when they first started dating, she'd try her hardest to make David keep a condom on, but he wouldn't listen. When he'd fuck her from the back, he'd rip the tip of the condom and act like it popped, trying to get her pregnant. Poca loved him and was hurt that he'd do a thing like that, and she had her reasons why.

So after their crazy night in the car, and massaging Poca's ego for a couple days, she finally gave in. She had Achuri whipped, fascinated by her swagger. It would be easy to get the blueprint. David instructed Poca to keep fucking with her, keep doing what she'd been doing.

When Poca told David about her he acted as if he was shocked. She explained everything about Achuri: the car shop, the garbage cans filled with pills and money. They were so loaded with cash they had to count with money counters. David's eyes grew large like a crackhead, all he could envision were dollar signs. David could hear the money talking, could see it and, most of all, could smell it. Poca explained to him the situation, that the Asian Gang were deadly, nothing to fuck around with. The Asian Gang rolled deep, and one would seldom see them by themselves. Everywhere they went they were at least ten deep. They would pull up on black motorcycles, wearing black glasses, showing their honor, loyalty, and strength. Poca knew the shop was where they kept a lot of their money and drugs, and it was also where they did their business.

One day Achuri invited Poca to an extravaganza, an expensive seafood buffet on the coast. It was a high end, very expensive restaurant; the place laced in fancy Asian attire. They pulled up and got out of the car. Achuri gave the valet attendant a fifty dollar bill and he parked the car for her. The inside of the restaurant was decorated with maroon and gold ancient Asian vases lining the doorway. The portraits that hung on the walls were worth hundreds of thousands of dollars. The waiters were all petite, beautiful, and none of them understood English.

Poca was surprised, thinking that she was going to the usual Chinese restaurant they ate at. She thought she would see a normal array of food, such as lobster, crabs and shrimp fried rice. When Poca read through the menu she thought, *what the fuck, Mami!* Her stomach bubbled as she saw what was on the menu. Poca looked up, almost puking as a fat Asian woman ate a fried tarantula. They were at an exotic Asian restaurant, only for the powerful Asians in their society, where you had to have a membership to get inside. There were exotic animals shipped from all over the world: tarantulas, octopus, shark meat, baked scorpion, fried Kangaroo, and multiple other animals.

Achuri laughed, telling Poca they had regular food on the other side of the menu. Poca was disgusted and didn't want to eat anything; all she wanted was a glass of wine and to get the hell out of there. Poca was all the way turned off by Achuri now; her beauty was the only thing she could stand. She was tired of the whole girl on girl thing. This wasn't the lane she was used to driving in. Knowing she was uncomfortable, Achuri whistled to the waitress for the check. The waitress left to get the check.

"Are you okaym baby? I thought this would be different and you'd enjoy it," Achuri said.

"It's okay, mami. It was just something new for me."

The waitress came back with the check and handed it to Achuri. Achuri gave her a fifty dollar bill and told her to keep the change. They got out of their chairs, pushing them in, and walked toward the door. Achuri said bye to a couple of people she knew, grabbed Poca by the hand, and walked her to the car. Achuri started the engine of her car, put it in drive, and pulled off.

Poca already had a blunt rolled up that she wanted to spark to get her mind right. Grabbing a lighter from her leopard Hermes purse, she put the tip of the blunt to her mouth and inhaled, the taste of the exotic marijuana overwhelming. She coughed and coughed as the smoke traveled through her lungs. They both laughed and continued driving down the highway.

Poca started thinking about what her and David discussed. She really didn't want to do it at first, but the money hadn't come yet from her mother, and something happened with the lawyers. She was still waiting for all that to clear up so she could have her money. She thought about it long and hard. This would be a big lick and they needed the money! Poca hadn't been to the shop at night yet, only in the evenings. She wanted to know what was going on, how many people ran the shifts, and what people were normally there on a regular basis.

After the blunt was finished, Poca told Achuri to pull over. She wanted to wipe the blunt guts off of her dress. Poca already knew how to get her pussy wet, tickle her ego, and keep squeezing her ass. She got out of the car and Achuri followed, both staring at the beautiful water. The boats were large lighting up the sky over the darkness of the ocean. Poca started playing with Achuri, talking to her in a Spanish accent. She smacked and squeezed her ass, talking dirty to her.

"I want you to suck my pussy, and you better do it good, mami. I ain't playing with you," Poca said, grabbing her by the hair.

Achuri became aroused. She had a new dildo at home and wanted to try it at her house.

Poca told her that her house was too far and, why not fuck somewhere they never fucked before? The car shop was fifteen minutes away. "Mami, lets fuck on top of one of your uncle's car. I love the Monte Carlo!"

"I don't know, baby. What if somebody there? Though normally there's no one there on Friday nights. Every Friday they go to the bike races to show off their sick wheels on the other side of town!" Achuri said.

It was Friday. Poca figured it was a good night to inspect the car shop. Achuri knew she only had a couple hours before her family got back. She didn't want to get busted because they already told her to never bring someone who wasn't Asian there again.

Poca was very persuasive, so fifteen minutes later they pulled up to the car shop. Achuri parked the car and they both got out. The thrill of getting caught had her excited—she loved to be spontaneous. They walked up to the side door and Achuri put the alarm code in. Poca watched, remembering it easily, acting as if she wasn't paying attention. Achuri turned the alarm off and they both walked inside. Achuri was rolling off of a pill and so was Poca. Achuri was hot, wearing next to nothing, showing her flawless skin.

Being flirty, she asked Poca, "Do you like my new tattoo?"

Achuri turned the music on and started giving her a lap dance. Poca was sucking her breast, sliding her fingers up and down the side of her waist. They both had on cute dresses, high heels, looking flawless.

236

Poca slid down her panties, pulling one leg out at a time, spinning her panties on her finger as if she was on a horse with a rope trying to catch the bull. She turned Poca around, kissing her on every curve of her body.

The whole time Poca couldn't stop thinking about David. She wasn't feeling the whole girl thing; it was just a phase for her, something new to keep her occupied while she waited for her love. Achuri made Poca spread her legs apart and poke her ass in the air. She stuck her finger inside of her and started sucking on her clitoris. Achuri was okay at giving head. She wasn't terrible, but she wasn't the best. Poca got what she came for, she got the alarm code, and now she knew that Friday was the night to hit.

Achuri still tasted every inch of Poca's body. Once she made her orgasm, she was ready to go; she didn't want to get caught by her family. The situation could get ugly, it could get out of her hands, meaning they wouldn't let her leave.

Achuri nervously turned the alarm on and they both walked outside of the car shop. They got in Achuri's car, shutting the doors. Achuri started the car up and they pulled off, both satisfied. Poca laid the seat back and closed her eyes as Achuri drove her to her car. Poca was exhausted, in need of a nap. She couldn't wait to get home to her man. Achuri and her both knew this was maybe the last time they'd see each other.

As they were pulling closer to the restaurant, a group of black motorcycles started flashing their high beams. Achuri looked in the rearview mirror, squinting to see what was going on. Once she realized it was her cousins, she pulled over in the plaza a block away. She rolled down her window as three of her cousins got off of their bikes. They took their black helmets off and started walking toward the car.

Poca awakened, realizing that they'd pulled over. She looked up and saw three Asian men at her window. They were speaking in their language so she couldn't understand what they were saying. All she knew was that they didn't sound too friendly. She quickly fixed her chair leaning it all the way up. She grabbed her purse where she knew her gun was at because she felt uncomfortable. The three Asian men all looked inside of the car at Poca, and she didn't know what to think. Achuri started raising her voice, getting angrier. The three Asian men laughed and walked away. One of them came back, smiling and saying something to her. He looked at Poca again and caught up with his cousins. They put their helmets on, got onto their bikes, and pulled off. As they pulled off, Achuri raised her middle finger at them.

She looked at Poca and said, "Sheesh, they get on my nerves."

Poca was curious to know what was going on because it was weird to her. "What was that about, mami?"

"My big cousins still think that they're in Asia. They don't like for Asians to fraternize outside of our culture. It's not just you; it's anyone I bring around who isn't Asian. I never been like them. I always had a diverse group of friends and my family knows it. I don't care what they talking about anyway. I'm grown, and I can hang with whoever I want."

"So what did the tall one say when he looked at me and laughed?" Poca asked.

"Who Miyawo? Oh, he crazy, girl, don't mind him. He thinks he's some gigolo or something." Achuri said.

"Well, what did he say?"

"At first, they were mad that I didn't come to my little cousin's first bike race. Then my cousin, Miyawo, said that you was a cute girl, and that he wanted your number. He's more like me—he had a white girlfriend before. I love him. He is, and always will be, my favorite cousin."

CHAPTER 29

THE HUNTED

Tired of running

Poca and David were preparing to relocate, having it set in their minds to leave California immediately. Poca had a gut feeling that something bad was getting ready to happen. She wasn't concerned about the furniture at her place. She was ready to leave and get the hell out of California as soon as possible.

While she was at the restaurant telling the workers that she was closing down the shop, one of the workers told her that a black limo had been suspiciously been lingering around the area for a couple days. Poca raised her eye brows, getting into complete thought mode. With all that was going on, she forgot that her brother told her the mafia knew of their location. Getting nervous walking to the window, she opened the blinds slightly just to check and see if something was out the ordinary. As she was closing the blinds, a black limo pulled up on the other side of the street and parked. Poca hadn't been at the restaurant in four days and the workers said they noticed the limo five days ago. The mafia was on their top heavy, more angry than before. They had been circling the area waiting to catch her and her brother slipping. The first thing that came to mind was where her brother could be.

David and Danny were at the apartment packing up the last bit of things they were taking. They were on their way back to the restaurant to pick up Poca, when suddenly Danny's phone rang.

"Danny, one of the workers said that a black limo has been circling the area for five days. The same limo is parked across the street, sitting there right now."

Poca's brother already knew what time it was, what was getting ready to happen. He started speeding, weaving through traffic. Luckily, they were only ten minutes away. David knew something was wrong. He could tell by her brother's vibe and how he was driving. David didn't ask any questions or say a word. He took his gun off his waist, cocking the hammer back and flipped off the safety. Poca's brother looked at him with a respectful eye, saluting that he was riding. They pulled up at the back of the store, putting together a plan. Poca came out back and they all started strategizing

"We can sneak up on them from the blind side. I'm tired of these motherfuckers. The chase ends now," Danny said.

They crept around the corner from the opposite direction, all of them scooting down so as not to be spotted. David gave a Mexican kid twenty dollars to ask the mob guys for directions as a distraction. The kid walked over to the car and started knocking on the window. Both of the men started screaming at the kid to get away from their car. It was the mafia. The Mexican kid stuck his tongue out, running away to play with his friends again. They were playing soccer, kicking the ball and bouncing it on their heads like Lionel Messi.

Poca and her brother were tired of this war and were ready to die trying to end it. Poca started thinking about her dead father and family, and at that point she lost it. David saw her facial expressions, saw her becoming angrier, and had to think quickly. David watched Poca getting ready to attack.

Without any hesitation, she came running from the blind side blasting. She wasn't thinking, not realizing she must save her ammunition. With only one clip and half the bullets gone, the only thing on her mind was revenging her lost ones. David was shocked, turned on—nothing better than a woman that's war ready. David ran the opposite way, strategically thinking. While Poca and her brother had their attention, shooting and taking cover, he'd sneak the other way and ambush them from the back side. David darted around the back, running full speed. He had no time to waste. Poca and her brother's lives were on the line.

Poca and her brother were both firing their weapons, aiming for the windows and gas tank. The men got out of their car and took cover, firing back with large automatic weapons. A brigade of bullets ripped through the car they were taking cover behind. They were fully prepared for the war.

"Wooo they got some heat, sister."

Danny hit one of mafia guys in the chest. He didn't stop, he didn't fall, and he wasn't fazed. "They wearing bullet proof vests! Aim for the neck and head," Danny yelled.

The mafia guys were loaded with more ammo, more power, and their job was to murder. The street was crowded; the little kids still playing as if they were used to it. They just took their game down the street, waiting for the commotion to be over. Everyone started taking cover, running, falling, trying not to be hit by stray bullets. The shootout lasted ten minutes as they ran out of ammo.

"I'm out of bullets, bro."

"Me, too. Where the fuck did David go?" Poca's brother asked.

They ducked behind a truck. Without any ammo left, they thought their time was up. Danny took a peek around the car. Their enemy was switching clips and walking toward them.

"Sis, we have to make a run for it. They're coming to us. David, that motherfucker. I'm-a kill him for abandoning us."

The mafia men were getting ready to finish the job once and for all. Just as Poca and Danny were getting ready to make a run for it, David was tip toeing low to the ground. He snuck up behind the two mafia men closest to Poca and her brother, and pointed the gun at their heads, firing twice. The men fell to the ground lifeless. David stood over them, breathing hard, emptying his clip into their face. He then ran over to Poca and Danny, praying and hoping that neither one of them ate slug.

"Poca, Poca. Where y'all at?"

Poca and her brother came out of cover and walked toward David, relieved. When they saw the two men lying on the ground with blood coming out of their heads, they both were surprised and now understood why he just ran off. Poca was staring at her King, her hero, the man who just saved her and Danny's life. She jumped in his arms with joy and appreciation, knowing he would never abandon a war. Poca's brother hugged him and felt bad for ever thinking otherwise.

"Amazing, soldier. Much respect. That was some G shit how you took those puntas out."

David looked up to salute him and saw two marked police cars. The officers jumped out with their guns. "Freeze! Let me see your hands."

David wasn't taking a chance; he just came home and was trying to keep it that way. He turned around and started shooting at the cops.

"Go get the car ready and pull down the block a little. I'm-a hit the alley way, go now!"

The two cops opened fire. There were only two of them, so their aggression was light. David had four bullets left as he turned around shooting, and hit the alley way for dear life. He felt bullets whizzing past him, missing by inches. He jumped in the car and they pulled off calm, appearing normal. Cops were flying up the street, car after car looking for a black male on foot. This was fun for David who sat in the back seat laughing, as Poca and her brother looked at each other, thinking, *This motherfucker crazy!*

Poca was relieved that no one was killed! She never got a chance to put a For Sale sign up in the window and shut the restaurant down. She figured fuck it. After speaking to the lawyers two nights ago, she was pleased to know that the funds from her mother were now transferred to her bank account. She never told David about her financial situation, but planned on surprising him once they made it to PA. She wanted badly to tell David, wanted to tell him he didn't have to pull the lick. But she couldn't just yet, wanting to see if he was all the way down for her.

David and Poca's brother were bonded now after the shootout. They were back on their original mission, robbing the car shop and getting out of California. They desperately needed the money now, so they started putting a plan together. They had the alarm codes, the date, the time; all they could see were dollar signs.

It was Thursday night and Poca didn't feel comfortable staying at her house. She and David went and got a hotel room. David tossed and turned, sweating through the night. He spent most of his nights that way. Every night his eyes closed, he'd visualize the faces, the souls of his victims he slaughtered. In his dreams, all the victims were impatiently waiting for him at the end of the tunnel for their vengeance. Poca would hold him tightly, wondering what he was going through.

David woke up and walked to the bathroom. Poca was asleep, snoring, looking like a Spanish princess. David opened the door and grabbed a wash rag. He put it beneath the hot water to let it soak. He took the cloth, squeezing the water out, and then looked in the mirror as he wiped his face with the rag. Every thought, every feeling came back to him. He regained his memory fully and was now all the way back to his normal thought process. Being in a coma and losing his memory—those two years in state prison only made him more deadly, stronger, and fiercer. He knew his past couldn't be changed; no matter what he was or who he was.

David prayed to the Lord, *I would never pass this poison to an innocent woman again*.

As he started thinking about the condom breaking when he was fucking Poca, his stomach filled with butterflies. Throwing up last night's meal made him realize there was a chance he could have given her HIV. David brushed his teeth, rinsing his mouth out with Listerine. He turned the light out and kissed Poca on the forehead, telling her that he loved her, and fell back to sleep.

CHAPTER 30

SKELETONS

Done in the dark

It was morning and David was out of bed, still on a prison time schedule. He was doing pushups on his knuckles and a stomach exercise Poca had never seen before. She knew David was getting ready to put that work in. She had a gut feeling, a funny vibe— something was telling her things would go wrong. It seemed too easy, too simple, and for them to be a vicious family, why would they leave their money unprotected? It was just fishy to her and she could smell the tartar sauce. She didn't want to lose her last brother or the man of her dreams.

Poca smoked all day, thinking about how she could stop them from robbing the car shop. She had to come up with something good. David and her brother wouldn't listen to her and they already had the blueprint in motion. The hours were quickly passing, and Danny was on his way over to their hotel room. David and Poca hurriedly dressed as he continuously knocked on the door.

Poca's brother was dressed in all black militant ready for the mission. David fucked with her brother heavy; he liked the way he operated. David was always ready, trained to go, all day every day.

"What's up, my boy? You ready to get this money, bra?" David said.

"Am I family? I was born ready. Let's go in here and take everything we can."

Poca looked at her clock, realizing she had only a few hours to convince them not to rob the car shop. She already gave them the blueprint, told them the passcode, the directions, and what time the races started. She knew Achuri felt the vibe between them. Poca was now unsure if she alerted her family to be on point on Fridays. It was possible they'd start leaving someone there in case anyone tried to get into the shop.

An hour passed and the time was now. Poca looked at the clock again and started thinking, *I'm-a just tell him that I have a lot of money and we can leave for PA NOW to get his daughter.* Poca called David inside of her bedroom away from her brother.

"Danny, give us like twenty minutes. We really need to talk about something," Poca said.

She didn't know the right way to tell him, but she had to get it off her chest before went any further. Poca wanted to tell him everything from A to Z, and she hoped, she prayed, that God would help him understand.

"David, there is something I have to tell you. Baby, roll this weed up and give me your ears for a second. Before I left Puerto Rico and moved to PA, I once had a beautiful life. My mother, two brothers, and my father spoiled me rotten. My father was getting major money, working for the Spanish mafia. He wanted out of the game, tired of it, eventually wanting to get away from it all. When he tried to get out, they killed him and put a hit on me and my family. Papi, I know this sounds crazy, and the only reason I'm telling you this is because I know that you love me."

"What, babe, spit that shit out. Don't beat around the bush. You know I'm an understanding man," David said.

"When I was a young girl, only thirteen years old, I was messing with my older brother's friend. My father would've killed him if he knew, so we kept it a secret."

"Yeah, yeah. Okay, so what happened?" David said.

"He took my virginity, heart, and spirit all at the same time. I was devastated, crushed, and way too young to play with love." David wiped the tears from her face, waiting for her to finish her story.

"When I told my mother what happened, she promised not to tell my father. She lied and did anyway and he went bananas, beating me, punishing me, and then submitting me to the doctors to be tested. They took my blood, my urine, and gave me a physical. When all of my results came back—" Poca started crying. "—they told me, they told me...that I was HIV positive."

"What? What the fuck they tell you?" David yelled.

"That I was HIV positive."

"What the fuck you mean HIV positive? Bitch, you better be joking!"

Poca ran out of the room in shame, in fear. She told her brother to grab the keys and get ready to leave.

David stood there shocked, confused, frustrated, and getting angrier by the second. Everything was starting to come back. He paced back and forth. David's body grew hot, feeling like razor pins raised beneath the surface of his skin. As thoughts raced through his head, he realized she'd been infected when she came to America.

David thought, *What the fuck? She got HIV. I can't believe this shit.*

He knew he'd dealt with her before Cream, thinking, *If she had HIV the whole time, then she was the one who infected me*! He fell to his knees, screaming at the top of his lungs, crying as every memory came back. He opened his soulless eyes at his murderous hands.

"Cream, Portia, Mike, Smalls, Danielle, all died for nothing. This whole war was for nothing," David said.

He was furious, trying hard to control his rage. He didn't know what to think, how to feel, or what to do. All these years he was under the impression Cream gave him HIV, and the whole time it was Poca. *What would you do if the love of your life was the one who gave you HIV?* David wiped the tears from his eyes, promising to never shed a tear again. He put his black lochs on and walked out of the room. He didn't want to let Danny see him in an emotional state. David walked out noticing that he'd left. He figured Poca dropped him off, so she could come back home for them to really converse.

He was in need of a blunt and a shot of liquor. He was trying his hardest not to grab his gun.

I should kill her and her brother. Fuck that!

Sitting on the edge of his bed with his gun in his hand, he waited for Poca to come back. David thought about prison, how the old head pimp would tell him to think three steps ahead before moving. He started thinking to calm himself down, but it was hard. Poca was all he had left; now a strong force in his life. David couldn't accept that she'd given him HIV. He thought, how could he even consider sparing her life? After all of the innocent lives that he took, all the innocent women he passed HIV to, he couldn't believe he got it from Poca.

Poca pulled up to the hotel and parked the car. She didn't know what to think or how David was going to react.

"Fuck it." With nothing to lose she walked inside. Putting down her purse, she looked side to side, figuring David would be in the bathroom.

David came out with a frown, gun in his hand, and a tear rolling down his cheek. He walked over to Poca and put his hand around her neck, squeezing. Confused about what to do, a million things sped through his mind. Poca started crying, telling him she'd die without a fight if he decided to kill her. David thought back when they were young lovers, and couldn't do it. He slowly loosened his hands from around her neck. Even though he still wanted war and blood, he believed in the Lord more than ever and always begged for his forgiveness. David loved Poca from the moment he laid eyes on her—she was the woman of his dreams. He thought about it over and over again, thinking, *we could live the rest of our lives together!* David weighed his pros and cons, feeling relieved. All the blood he'd spilled was now drying.

"There's no point in me telling you my life story since you left. All I can say is that my hands are bloody, my spirit is soulless, and I have demons that stalk my dreams every night. I am a dead man walking; there will be no growing old with gray hair for me. You killed me Poca. For all of the blood I spilled, it lies on your hands now. I'm going to forgive you, mami, and one day we will be able to move past this and live together forever, forget our past and bless our future," David said.

Poca started sobbing, listening to every word David spoke. She always wondered if he did have it, and what he would do once he found out. Every word stung, pierced her heart like a heart attack.

Poca got up and stared David in the eyes. "Papi, I am so sorry for what I've done—there are no words that can explain my love for you. I will never leave you, will never let another man lay a hand on me. Look, I was going to tell you not to do the job, Papi. My mother left me two hundred grand. I can take care of you until it's your time to shine. We can go anywhere to start all over, start a business. Let's go and get your daughter, Papi. I'm riding with you. Let's kill whoever has her."

They decided not to go through with the job. Poca convinced David to go straight to PA to kill King and take his daughter back. They booked their flights and flew out the next morning. Poca kissed California goodbye, not even saying good bye to Achuri or anyone. They made it to the John Wayne Airport. Poca reserved two furnished condos downtown by the Susquehanna River for two months. One for her and David and one for her brother. She had everything put together.

CHAPTER 31

LONG FLIGHT

A soldier returns

They were boarding the airplane to PA, which was humongous, having bed seats for the long flight. They sat in their assigned seats, putting their seat belts on. The airplane was filled to capacity, with different cultures from all over the world. Danny was a ladies man, and thought every girl desired him. He was loved and treated special by all the girls. As they were being seated the, female flight attendant couldn't keep her eyes off of him. Every time she walked past his isle, she would flirt and compliment him. He loved the attention trying to show off for his new brother-in-law.

A couple hours passed and the lady flight attendant walked by again. She gave him a letter and told him to read it.

"*Meet me in the bathroom in thirty minutes, you are hot and I want to fuck you.*"

He smiled with excitement, being a hundred percent with it. Danny couldn't wait, and loved having sex in weird places. He told Poca what was going down. She didn't believe him, so he showed her the letter. Danny took the seat belt off and got out of his chair. Feeling lucky, he started combing his hair in a ponytail as he walked to the restroom. After having problems dating women in California, he was easily aroused and ready to enjoy this exhilarating moment.

The door opened up and it was her. Immediately, they started kissing. She pulled his pants down and began giving him oral pleasure. She was a pretty, blonde haired white girl in her early twenties, with light brown eyes. She pulled her hair back into a ponytail using a rubber band to wrap it. She didn't want it to keep getting in her face while she worked her magic. She used both hands to massage his erect penis, sucking it softly as if she'd been doing it her whole life. She was sucking his penis like she needed it, like she hadn't sucked dick in years.

One thing Danny hated was a girl who couldn't suck dick. A girl who sucked dick and always tried to deep throat it, but couldn't. One that squeezed it too hard, too rough, point blank just didn't know what they were doing. Danny was enjoying the oral pleasure

256

thinking, *this bitch right here!* He leaned his head back and put his hands on top of her head. She was working her hands and her mouth all at the same time. She wore a navy blue Flight attendant suit and her skirt was well fitted. She pulled down her white and navy blue panties and lifted up her skirt.

Danny started kissing her neck as she turned around for him to fuck her doggy style. The first thing that Danny would do before he had sex with a female was open her vagina lips and smell the pussy. She smelled like clear spring water, a pure aroma that he liked. He ripped the condom out of the package and put it on, making sure that it was on properly. He grabbed both of her butt cheeks and spread them open, smacking her ass lightly as he pulled her hair. He spit in his hand and started rubbing on her already moist vagina. Danny grabbed his cell phone and started recording as he penetrated inside of her. Thinking, *World Star lol.* She covered her mouth, trying her hardest not to let the entire plane hear her moaning. Danny was going in and out, out and in. She was super wet every time he went inside of her that it felt as if the condom was off. He was fucking her good, stroking nice and gentle, trying not to be heard.

He stopped hitting it from the back and sat her on the counter of the sink. Danny put her legs over top of his shoulder, as she rubbed her clitoris in a circular motion. The angle he was fucking her in was hitting her spot perfectly. He could feel the inner walls of her pussy attacking him like he was a piece of meat. She loved his dick for the moment, rubbing her hand

257

through his ponytail and squeezing his ass. Just as she was coming so was he.

Danny took the condom off and threw it in the toilet and flushed it. He pulled his pants up, exchanged info with her, and walked back to his seat smiling. Poca was asleep, so Danny took his seat quietly, so as not to disturb her.

Close to PA, the weather was terrible and running into a small storm. The sky became grayer by the second; the clouds gloomy and thin. Thunder could be heard rumbling like an empty stomach. The ride was rough, windy, bumpy, and the turbulence was almost too much to handle. David hated flying; hated heights and wished he could take a sleeping pill and wake up when they arrived. All of the passenger's faces could be seen, looking side to side to see if anyone was panicking. The plane shook so much that it woke Poca and Danny up from their rest.

"What the fuck, papi? This fucking airplane is out of control," Poca said.

"I don't know, but this isn't feeling right. I am not feeling this shit, cuz," Danny said.

The airplane hit an air bubble, making it drop twenty feet in midair. Everyone on the plane started screaming and yelling, praying, and hoping they weren't going to crash. Poca's brother held on to the sides of the chairs, praying in his head to the Lord. Everyone feared for their lives, crying, and kids were petrified and screaming loudly. The plane stopped shaking and dropped another twenty feet, the engines turned off, and the aircraft was smoking heavily. The plane was falling fast from the sky, the oxygen masks dropping from the ceiling. The passengers were yelling to put their masks on. The pilot must have had God on his side still trying to steer the plane. The plane was falling from the sky nose first, spinning in a circular motion. The engines were now on fire and the strong winds ripped the roof off of the plane. The passengers were all flying out of their chairs, Poca and Danny trying their hardest to hold on. They tried their hardest until eventually the merciless winds snatched their bodies away.

Just as the plane was getting ready to hit the ground and explode, David woke up.

It was all a dream.

He woke up panting, shivering, and looking around to realize everyone still sat in their seats. David relaxed as he caught his breath, calming down. The same attendant who just had sex with Poca's brother came over to him asking him if he was alright.

"I'm straight. Just had a bad dream." David got out of his seat and walked to the restroom. Apparently the plane must have been having some bad turbulence. Over the loud speaker, the pilot told everyone to relax, that it was just an air bubble. They were thirty minutes from the Harrisburg airport and everyone on the airplane couldn't wait for the plane to land.

CHAPTER 32

HARRISBURG

Commonwealth

They made it to Harrisburg safe and sound. When they got off of the airplane, they headed to their reserved black Yukon. David smiled as they got closer to the city that wanted his head on a platter. By all means, he didn't want to be spotted, not wanting King to be alerted that he was in the area. First things first, he had to go down York to Danielle's old house. He hoped and prayed that his spare gun was still stashed in the back yard. He'd buried it for a rainy day.

On the ride from the airport, Danny was stone-faced the whole time. He was a little upset they'd done all of that homework and didn't pull the heist out in Cali. When David came through and saved their lives, he had a much greater respect for him. So he was

1

wanting and willing to help his brother-in-law go to war.

They pulled into the city and got off of the Eisenhower Boulevard exit. They stopped at the Sunoco to get a couple of things for the room: blunts, cookies, bottled water, and soap. They got back on the highway heading toward downtown Harrisburg to their Condos. There was a cop parked across the street with his radar watching traffic. They drove the speed limit, continuing on their mission.

When they arrived at their condo, Poca walked inside of the office and grabbed their keys. She gave her brother his and they all walked to their rooms. They were restless and in need of sleep from the long flight. They went straight to their rooms to get settled in. Poca and David decided to take a quick nap and chill for a minute from the long exhausting flight. There was one other thing David had to do, and that was to stop at Brandy's place, his old foster home.

David was nervous not knowing how they would react. How would they feel seeing him again? Poca gave him a thousand dollars and told him to make it work. He kissed her on the forehead and told her he'd be right back. He left the condo and went to the truck. There were girls all throughout the hotel, some tricking and some just staying the night there. There was a bike show that weekend, so people from out of town were coming in by the numbers. He made it to the truck, got in, and pulled off. David jumped on the highway because he hated driving through downtown, dealing with the Capital police. The police over there were racist pigs, and would pull you over for anything, especially a DWB, "Driving While Black."

David explained to Poca and Danny in full detail the danger of this operation. He knew he had to hit King a certain way, and it would not be easy. He couldn't just run inside of somewhere and kill him. He had to make sure he had his daughter first. For the first time in David's life, he was going to fight a war blind. He had no idea of King's locations, his allies, or his new affiliations. He had to do a sufficient amount of homework and back track to their old hangout spots, hoods, clubs, bars, and the whole nine.

This was a dark road and at the end of the tunnel there was not a good chance of light. David was a coldhearted murderer, twice as dangerous now. If there one thing that he knew it was how to get away with murder. He was on a murder hunt and, in his mind, revenge was sweeter than pussy. He was against all odds— him against the world. He was the underdog, the kid nobody wanted to play with.

I am going to kill every motherfucker that he love. Mom, sister, kids, even the dog dies! David hated King and everything he stood for, thinking, *This man just gone kidnap my daughter!* Every day David thought of King holding his daughter. The pain was unbearable, picturing King feeding her, bathing her, or whatever the situation was. David had no idea if she was dead, alive, healthy or what. He wore his war paint—Rambo, commando—prepared to go all the way out. His daughter was the only thing good, only thing pure, only reason he had to hold on to this worthless life. After all of the years wishing and hoping Poca would come back to him, David finally had his woman back.

After being gone for two years, pretty much everything in the hood had changed. David went to prison a boy and came home a grown man. He was happy to be free, but at the same time revenge clouded his mind. David parked the truck and saw an old associate across the street at the New York Fried Chicken. He had a few questions he needed to ask him. David looked side to side, back and front, making sure that he was on point.

"What's up, my boy? What's really good is I'm back out, chere."

"Oh shit what's up bra, I heard that you was on your way home."

"They can't keep a real killer down, my boy, but what's good? I know you been out here, so I know you know something. Where the fuck is King at with my daughter?"

"I don't know, bro. I don't even fuck with them like that no more. I just came back from living in Charlotte, North Carolina."

"Is that right? It's like that, my boy? Fuck out of here, bra. Now you don't fuck with them no more. As deep as you was, King would never let you walk these streets alive," David said.

David stepped away and kept it moving. He knew what the situation was hitting for. As soon as David turned his back, the guy pulled his cell from his pocket. He dialed King's number informing him of the conversation he had with David.

"OG, you know the boy, David, is home. I just seen him at the New York Fried Chicken. He asked me about his daughter or something, I played it off, my G."

"Oh yeah, that motherfucker home, dawg? I been waiting, waiting for a long time for this day, homie. I'm a hit you back. Let me send some folks over there. Little Queasy and Shell Mack just told me they were at the Speedway gas station on Cameron Street," King said.

"Alright cool."

David walked back across the street toward his truck.

"David, oh my God, is that you. Damn, you look good," a girl said.

"Oh shit, what's up, Dana? Damn, I see that ass got fatter. What you been up to?

"Same ole, same ole, raising these kids."

"What's your number? I'm-a call you on your phone. I'm in a rush, lil mamma."

David got her number and continued on his mission. He was still paranoid, but enjoyed life outside of prison walls. As David was walking to his car, he passed a bus stop noticing a *Know Your Status* campaign poster. There were mothers, kids, and elders all waiting for the public bus. It was a nice day with perfect weather, especially since it had been raining off and on for the whole week. Just as he was walking away a navy blue minivan pulled up, creeping, the windows darkly tinted. David immediately became alert knowing that it could go down at any moment.

The window rolled down and the side door of the van swung open. All David saw was fire coming out of the guns that were aimed at him. David fell to the ground grabbing a lady as a shield, *like Nino Brown did in the movie New Jack City*. He took cover behind a parked car, trying to get low. Bullets were ricocheting off of cars, buildings, and busting out windows. When the gun fire stopped, David heard screams, cries, and saddened voices. When he looked up, there was a little boy no more than four years old lying on the ground with his hand to his neck. Blood squirted out like a water fountain.

The kid's mother was screaming and crying, holding him in her arms trying her hardest to revive him. "Help, Help. Why the fuck are y'all not helping me? Someone call an ambulance. My baby is dying!" The little boy's body was lifeless; nothing the mother could do. David felt heartbroken seeing another innocent victim gone because of him.

He got up quickly, got into his car, and sped off.

CHAPTER 33

FOSTER MOM

Eye of the killer

David's mind was racing all day to figure out his next moves. After the drive by shooting, he wasn't going nowhere in public until he went down to York to get his pistol. These last couple of nights had been restless for him. He'd been tossing, turning, and sweating through each night. The symptoms from his illness were starting to become more prevalent. The past couldn't be changed no matter who he was, his inner demons crippling him every time he thought of his life.

He continued driving up to Brandy's house, seeing if they still lived there. He hadn't spoken to or seen his foster mom in years. His stomach bubbled in fear of what lied in front of him. Parking the truck, he

1

got out and stared at the house, looking it up and down with a smile as memories surfaced. Muttering "*fuck it*" beneath his breath, he walked onto the porch.

He rang the doorbell and stepped back to see if someone looked out of the window. The curtain moved, it was Brandy's mother. She looked at David as if she'd seen a ghost. He wondered if she'd open the door or not. Once he heard the door unlocking he knew now was the time to face the mother of the son he slaughtered. She came to the door with a look on her face that David wasn't expecting.

"David!" she screamed, running over to give him a hug, showing him she missed him. She always loved David, but due to the circumstances with her daughter, she had to send him to a different foster home.

"David, baby, where have you been? It's been so long, look at you, you're all grown up now. Come inside. How are you? I see you gained some weight. Damn, boy, you look like a grown man. That's good. You're taking care of yourself? It's been crazy in the city. These young people just never learn. They out here killing each other every day left and right. It's at the point now they shooting at the cops. I tried to tell Smooth to leave them streets alone or one day they'll take his life. He wouldn't listen to me. I miss him so much. He was a good child, just misguided. That was a rough year for me. And you believe they tried to convince me you had something to do with it?"

She looked up at David, watching his reactions, gestures, and seeing if he got nervous.

"What? I haven't heard that yet. Smooth is my brother. I would kill for him. He gave me a beginning out here. Why would I take his life, mom? I looked up to Smooth from the first time I met him. I would never do that."

"I know, baby. I never believed them. It was probably something he had going on with his baby mom's brother, King. King is a killer. The police have been questioning him for murders from ten years ago. I told him to stay away from King, I told him he was bad business, but he wouldn't listen to me. King done shot some young kid up that was only fourteen years old. Now he stays uptown. That's all you hear about is King nowadays. I would 've thought the feds would've got him."

Brandy's mother loved to converse, and would talk forever if you allowed her to. David got a little information, not a lot, but it was more than what he had. She told him that Brandy moved to Dallas, Texas with her husband a couple months ago. David gave her a big hug saying that he loved her and would stay in touch with her.

He walked out of the house feeling morally better. He wanted to stop and get some weed for Danny; Poca had snuck hers on the airplane. He continued driving down Derry Street looking to see if someone would be in front of the all-nighter store. Young boys would be there hustling 24/7 with weed, heroin, and that hard "crack."

He got a quick quarter sack and pulled off, blasting his stereo to Young Jeezy. He pulled up to his old hood and saw familiar faces. He didn't want anyone to know he was home from prison, hiding behind the tint as he drove through. David had seen the same people wasting away in the hood. Nothing had changed but the weather. It was the same old crack heads, same dope fiends, and thirsty bitches walking around looking for their next baby daddy— everyone just seemed to have gotten older. All of the girls who were too young to get fucked were now ready. Their asses were fatter than the older girls, and the older dudes were dicking all of them down. They were out there mobbing, fucking, robbing the life that Harrisburg offered.

David continued driving down Hummel street and watched as a group of thugs shot dice on the corner. The block was packed, popping, people was rolling up blunts and having fun. The traffic came to a stop, it was two cars in front of David holding the street up. David wondered what was happening and quickly pulled through a side street. He couldn't be in Harrisburg without a gun with enemies and gangsters that wanted his life.

When he made it to York, David pulled up to Danielle's old house and saw that it was vacant. His memories came back instantly. A tear trickled down his cheek as he walked toward the back of the house. He went directly to the spot which now had tall weeds and bushes all around it. He used his powerful hands to pull the bushes out of the ground, so he could see if the gun was still there. After all these years, through snow, rain, and vicious winter storms, it would be a miracle if it was still there. David started flipping up the dirt with both of his hands. As he got deeper into the ground, he started feeling the wooden box he put it in. As he pulled the box out of the dirt, he showed the biggest smile. He wiped off all of the dirt and opened up the shoebox. David pulled the chrome .45 with the pearl handle out of the box and put it on his waist. He walked back to the truck and got inside.

"Oh shit, I forgot how fucking sexy this pistol was," David said to himself.

He pulled off on his way back to Harrisburg. There was no time to waste—David wanted to stab in and stab out. He was sneaky, always thinking of a way to get away with everything he did. The number one rule to war was never being visible, never letting your enemy see you coming. David lived and abided by these rules.

When it's time for war, the only time I'm coming outside is when I'm on a murder hunt.

The streets of Harrisburg feared him, respected him, through all the fucked shit, he was a goon. Everyone knew he was a stick up kid, a loose screw. King knew what type of shit he was on, and would now be more prepared for his arrival.

CHAPTER 34

CHESS MOVES

Three steps ahead

A week passed and David was tired of playing games. He was ready to go out blasting, robbing anything to get him closer to his daughter. He knew he didn't have much time now that King knew he was in town. He was asking around, searching for David's whereabouts, so he couldn't chance him doing anything to his daughter. David was creeping and covering the entire city of Harrisburg in hopes of finding Devunyae. David was staking out, watching all of their old hang out spots. He knew that eventually something or someone would lead him in the right direction. He had no idea who was getting money or who was running shit now because he'd been out of the loop for two years.

King had his guard up, alerting his allies and comrades to keep both eyes open. David stopped at a corner store to purchase a box of vanilla Dutch's. Since he'd been maxed out, he was smoking exotic weed every day.

I know where his sister live. Yeah, her ass is mine. I wanted to fuck her anyway.

David was almost finished smoking his blunt, blowing a thick cloud of smoke into the air. He coughed, eyes watering from the potency of the exotic weed. He decided to pay King's sister a visit. David was willing to go all the way, taking the most heinous route to seek victory.

Pulling up to her neighborhood, he hoped she still resided there, circling the block three times before parking. He checked the area for anything strange, marked cars, anything that looked out of place. In back of the truck, where the windows were darkly tinted, he laid his seat all the way back, not wanting to be seen. The sun was falling, the moon rising, and the stars sparkled like glitter throughout the midnight sky. David thought like a lion or a pack of wolves—he would sit on his prey for days.

He started rolling up another blunt, getting bored, since nothing had moved. Looking through his binoculars, he zoomed in hoping to see something. Hours passed, with it now two in the morning and still nothing. After a few blunts to the head, David eventually became tired and fell asleep. With his gun on his lap, he snored, slobbered, and tossed, and turned in an attempt to get comfortable in back of the truck.

As the sun rose, the sounds of people hitting their car alarms and getting into their cars woke David. Wiping the slobber from his face, he picked up his binoculars again, smiling as he noticed the door of King's sister's house opening. Walking out, she held the door open and waited for her daughter to come out.

"Hurry up, girl. You slowpoke, you're already late."

Her daughter walked out next with her jacket halfway on. She held her book bag with one hand and her pink Cinderella lunch box in the other. David thought, *Damn, she got big as fuck.* They walked off of the porch heading to the car. Smooth's baby mom opened the car door and helped her daughter inside. They pulled off and David automatically assumed that she was dropping her off at school. David thought, *I'm-a break in through the back. When she get back home, I'll be waiting with a big dick and a smile.*

He knew this neighborhood too well and had already been in their house hundreds of times. David knew their house like the back of his hand. She used to be a welfare broad, one of them girls who lived off the system and never had a job. She was only a fat ass, pretty face, with no talent or brains. Her complexion was brown and she would wear little designed wigs to match her outfits. She had a nice round ass that wasn't very big, but it poked out. In high school, they'd call her Table Butt, because you could sit a cup on it.

"I'm-a rape this bitch and then take her life. Eye for an eye, my boy!"

It was early in the morning and everyone was either sleeping or working. David put his hoodie over his head and started walking the opposite way to the back of her house. His hands were covered with black gloves, his boots with black plastic bags. David was strategic, knowing the perfect way to get away with murder. No fingerprints, no evidence, no witnesses.

David stuck a bobby pin inside of the door lock and started working it easily—it was his expertise. As he got the door open, the only thing stopping him from making an entrance was a chain lock at the top of the door. David dug his muscular shoulder inside the narrow opening and pushed the door open quietly, snapping the lock. Walking into the house he looked side to side with his gun in his hand. He held it firmly with his finger on the trigger just in case he had to open fire.

The whole downstairs was empty. He already knew what he wanted and needed. He went straight to the house phone to see if he could find any of King's information. He started going through the mail for anything to get him closer to King. He looked through the drawers, beneath the couch pillows, anywhere he could find clues. When he lifted up one of the couch pillows, he found a baby nine millimeter with an infra-red beam.

David happily picked it up, taking the clip out to make sure it wasn't loaded. He smiled. *Damn, everybody got a gun now days!* He put the gun on his waist and continued searching for clues.

As he finished looking through the mail, he noticed something had been sent from the same last name as King. It was his mother's address. David smiled and put the letter in his back pocket. He sat there lamping in the shadows of the living room waiting for her to get back. David was chilling, not moving, and lying there in silence when he first heard squeaks coming from upstairs. Someone else was in the house and started walking down the steps.

Oh shit. What the fuck? Are you serious!

The person got to the last step, yawning. It was a man, someone she was fucking. He started walking toward the kitchen, wearing only boxers. As he walked past, it was like David had seen a ghost—he was surprised to see who it was. It was Smooths' worker, the one who was at the waffle house when they got them charges a few years ago. The same guy who helped stomp him into a four month coma.

I knew I was going to see one of them motherfuckers again.

As the man walked past, David came from his blind side and pointed the gun at the back of his neck. The man stopped instantly, lifting his hands into the air. He was terrified, trembling. David enjoyed and loved every minute of fear in the man's eye. It gave him an explosive rush of adrenaline.

"I told y'all to kill me. Y'all some stupid motherfuckers letting me live. It's crazy how the clock rotate, how the tables turn, motherfucker. I see you fucking my brother's baby mom. That's that hoe shit! Turn your faggot ass around, bra. I never liked you anyway, you pretty motherfucker," David said.

"David, is that you?"

"Yeah, it's me. Where the fuck is King at with my daughter, bitch? I'm not asking twice, bra. You got to three to tell me where she is or your face will look like a half moon!" David said.

"I don't know, man, I don't know."

"One, two..."

As David got to two, he shoved the gun deeper into the side of his neck.

"Okay, cuz, okay okay. Just don't kill me, fuck that, he staying uptown all the way down Sixth Street. You turn right onto Division Street and it's the yellow house on your right."

"See, out the county you was on that rah rah shit. Now you giving me info about your boss. You a bitch ass nicca. Matter of fact, give me your cell phone and tell me where his number at," David said in a threatening tone.

276

"It's...717...370-9734...That's the last number I have from him."

Before David said anything else, the man turned around and darted to the living room. He panicked and started lifting up the pillows on the couch. He lifted up all of the pillows and then realized his gun was gone. As David ran toward him, the man knew he was getting ready to die. David was much stronger and bigger. He snatched him up and wrapped his arms around his neck.

"Motherfucker, I was going to let you die a fast and easy death!"

David started choking him, applying more and more pressure. He tried to escape, but wasn't strong enough. David lifted him in the air and twisted his arms aggressively— imagine a male lion shaking the neck of a baby gazelle. David twisted again and his neck broke easily, giving a loud, audible snap. The man died instantly as David watched. David pulled him by the arms and dragged him, his head bouncing on every step as his lifeless body was taken to the basement. He covered his body with a blanket, hiding it in the darkness.

As he made it up the stairs, he heard someone coming into the house; Smooth's sister. She came back happy, in a good mood, not knowing anything that had happened. She ran upstairs yelling for her man, and when he didn't respond, she said to herself, "I know this nicca didn't leave without giving me no dick."

She walked downstairs looking for him; she noticed his clothes were still there. He would always play little games trying to hide and scare her, so she automatically assumed that was what he was doing. She sat on the couch, turning on the T.V. She was horny, pussy tingling, so she put on a porno. She took off all of her clothes and started playing with her pussy. It was shaved with a piercing on her clitoris. Her clitoris was fat, and her vagina lips sat out perfectly. She knew her man would join her any minute. She put her finger inside of her mouth and started sliding them in and out of her fat, wet, slippery vagina. Moaning loud, so her man could hear her, she knew he'd come and finish the job.

David watched as she masturbated, rubbing her clitoris with a toy. He was getting aroused by the beauty of her sensual voice. David was rock hard and was now ready to take control. She was laid out, stretched on the couch with all of her energy out of her. She had no choice but to doze off after she busted a nut. When she opened her eyes, she opened them to a ghost. When she saw David, her heart fell to the floor, almost having a heart attack.

"Shut the fuck up! If you scream, it's going to get real ugly. I just have to ask you a few questions. One, where the fuck is my daughter? Two, where the fuck is your brother with my daughter? I know you think I killed Smooth. Well, I did, bitch, and I'm going to kill you also if you don't cooperate."

She hopped up, covering her exposed body as fast as she could. She was startled, too scared to say anything. All she knew was that the man who killed her baby father was in her house with a gun to her face. David wanted to get straight to the point. He pulled duct tape out of his back pocket, taping her hands behind her back. He covered her mouth, so she couldn't yell, and taped her ankles, so she couldn't run.

He stared at her curvaceous body, enjoying the sight of his deceased brother's baby mom. David pulled a condom out of his pocket and pulled down his pants. He left his boxers on, so no pubic hair could be traced. She sat there crying, watching him, and already knowing what he was up to. He pulled his dick out and slapped her on the forehead with it. She clenched her face as she stared at the size of it. David put the condom on, rolling it all the way down to the bottom. Normally, he'd fuck her raw and try to give her HIV, but he was past that at this point of his life. Plus he knew there was a way they could trace him by semen— today's technology was a motherfucker.

"Now I'm one hundred percent sure you need some dick right now anyway. I watched you playing with that pussy. I heard it slurping from way over there. I don't want to have to take it, girl. You know I been wanting to fuck you anyway," David said.

She sat in the corner of the couch crying, trembling, and scared of what was going to happen next. She was a street bitch—it wasn't that he was raping her with a long, thick horse dick, it was what he was going to do when he was finished. She figured she was a grown woman and could handle a dick.

David walked over to her with his dick in his hand. He wanted to see her face every time he rammed his long, thick cock inside of her. He removed the tape from her legs, then spread them all the way back, propping a couch pillow beneath her. This technique made her pussy sit perfectly in the air. He spit on his hand to lubricate the condom and then pushed his dick inside of her moist vagina. When he stuck it inside of her, she inhaled deeply as if she was enjoying the penetration. David started stroking her, pounding her, fucking her deep and hard. He enjoyed watching his dick going in and out. When he noticed that she was moaning through the duct tape, he was wacked out.

I'm supposed to be raping this bitch, terrorizing her, and she enjoying this shit.

David was deep inside of her and felt her getting wetter with every stroke. Turning her around, he gripped her fat ass and smacked each butt cheek. He spread open her eagle wings and started fucking her from the back. David was killing her, not showing any remorse to her tight vagina. He continued fucking her till he busted a nut.

He left the condom on and put the gun to her face. "Damn bitch, you got some good pussy. I see why you had my brother all fucked up. Now call your fuck ass brother, hoe."

She looked at David with desperation and picked up her phone to call King. "Brother."

David snatched the phone from her. "What's up, fuck nicca? This is your worst nightmare, the ghost has come back to haunt you!"

"Who the fuck is this?" King said.

"David, motherfucker. You, I'm-a kill everybody, everyone that you know until I get my daughter back. I just fucked your sister, bra. She got some good pussy, my boy. Bra, I told you that you could never beat me at this war shit. Bitch, I dreamed of killing you. I want to kill you so bad my dick is hard!" David said

"Is that right? What the fuck you doing at my sister's, bitch? You touch her and this pretty little girl of yours will be hidden beneath the cement. Yeah, I got your daughter and I'm waiting for your bitch ass to come take her back. Where your nuts at? You have no heart. Won't even come take your own daughter back!"

"Oh yeah, is that right? Okay, watch this. Come here, you dirty little whore." He grabbed Trina by the hair. "Tell your brother that you love him, tell him that you love your life and you're scared to die."

As she started telling him that she loved him, David snatched the phone from her ear and knocked out her earring. "See you think it's a game, bra. I told you, I showed you, that I'm about that life. Now you have to listen to your little sister die motherfucker."

David put the gun to King's sister's head, asking him if he was listening. He wanted him to hear his sister die, wanted him to feel the pain for all that he had done to him. "Say good bye to your sister, my boy."

David kissed her on the forehead, and put a pillow over her face to stop the blood from splashing. He pulled the trigger twice, releasing two hollow tips to the front of her face. The holes in her face were small in the front, but bigger in the back.

King was screaming through the phone, raging that his sister had been murdered. "I'm a kill you, motherfucker," King said.

David ran out of the back door and walked back to his truck as if nothing ever happened. He knew that King wouldn't hurt a baby and, by now, he'd have gained a little feeling for her.

David headed back to the hotel to get Danny to tell him the war was on. They both got back into the truck and headed into the city. David used Map Quest to find King's mother's address. Time was of the essence.

David called King back an hour later. "Where the fuck you at with my Daughter? I want to see a picture of her right now. All I want is your respect and my daughter. All the blood you spilled? Your sister is nothing. Now we can end this war bloody or peaceful, open or closed caskets—you know I don't give a fuck. Don't make me do the unthinkable and pay your mom's house a visit, bra!" David yelled out her address.

"You ever say my mom's name again and I'm going to kill your little princess. I'm going to snap her little neck like a tooth pick. Damn, David, she looks just like you dog. I wonder if my dick can fit in her little bitty tight pussy," King said with a fake laugh to taunt David.

David's eyes watered as the words stung his heart. "Bra, you touch my daughter I swear to you I won't stop hunting the land until I terminate all that you love. I just pulled up at your mom's house. She lives really close to your sister."

The first thing that King thought about was his daughter being at his mom's house. He knew the power David would gain if he had his angel and mother. What he didn't know was that half an hour ago David already pulled up at King's mother's house, having sent Danny inside her home to get her. Poca's brother loved this shit, it was fun to him. He went inside Ms. Connie's crib like a true gangster. He kicked the door in sending it flying off the hinges. King's mother was doing Spirit's hair, King's daughter. Danny swiftly snatched both of them up and put the gun to Spirit's neck.

"Where is the money? I only ask once. No money, no life for her," he said in his Puerto Rican accent.

King's mother knew he was serious. She moved the living room table off of the carpet. She lifted up the carpet and started ripping up the floor boards.

Danny smiled, knowing a golden treasure lay beneath the panels. Every baller, shot caller, or boss has something tucked away at their mother's house for a rainy day. So when she threw him the book bag stuffed full of money, she already knew what time it was.

Danny escorted both of them out of the door and into the truck. When David saw that a little girl was with King's mom, he smiled knowing she had to be King's daughter because they looked identical.

Well what we have here? See a prime example of why God don't like ugly.

David looked up seeing Danny also had a black book bag slung over his shoulder. "Oh shit, my boy, what's that?"

"Look, I found a gift under the floor." Danny opened the bag and it was filled with all one hundred dollar stacks. At the least it had to be sixty to seventy grand in there.

They both smiled and dapped each other up. David gave him the duct tape and told him to wrap them up. David still had King on the line, not paying him any attention as he screamed through the phone.

"When I get my hands on you I'm going to skin you like a cat!" King yelled.

David laughed, smelling the fear and devastation in King's voice. He had the upper hand and he knew it.

King was speeding through traffic, driving around cars and almost hitting them. He was coming from the other side of Harrisburg, meaning he had no time to waste. The only thing on his mind was saving his mother and daughter. King called his cousin Terry on the other end, telling him to get over to his mom's ASAP. Terry stayed just off of Radnor and Fourth Street, so he could easily get there in less than five minutes. A BMW came speeding past, flying, down the street into Kings mom's driveway.

David saw the car coming around the corner and knew it was someone King sent or the man himself. He smiled as he drove right past them with his daughter and mom in the truck.

"Okay, bra. I see I got your attention now. You quiet. What's wrong? I know you're still on the phone. Well the game just changed, bitch. One sec, hold up, bra. Hey, my G, let the girl speak."

Danny took the tape from around Spirit's mouth. She was sitting there shivering, crying, and wishing that her father was there to save them.

"Yo, King, you listening, my boy? I got someone who wants to speak to you. I told you you weren't war ready," David said.

"Daddy, daddy, help!" Spirit yelled.

Danny put the duct tape back around her mouth because she was screaming at the top of her lungs. "You hear that? I got your daughter and your mother, motherfucker." David hung the up phone.

King hung up his phone, immediately calling his mother's cell to see if they were really kidnapped. When he called her phone and David picked up, he knew it was real.

"Motherfucker," King snapped.

"I have your daughter and mother, and this is what I want. I already took your book bag from the floor at your mom's crib, so on top of that I want another sixty grand and my daughter back. Then I will give you back your mother and your precious daughter. I don't have all day, my boy. Your money long, so I know you got it. You got two hours to meet my demands. Every minute after that I'm a stick my dick deeper into your daughter's tight little ass, then I'm going slit your mother's throat from ear to ear, nicca," David yelled and hung up the phone.

CHAPTER 35

WAR LOSSES

Every dog has a day

King was traumatized and angered, yet more upset with himself than anything. He never imagined putting his family in jeopardy or any harmful situation. He thought he was invincible, untouchable—his power blinded him, and that was his only weakness. He took life, broke up families, and sent crying mothers to funeral homes. Karma is every soldier's fear, and King had crossed the line and knew it. He was finally the man on the other side of the gun line; the roosters had come back to hen.

King crossed town in his tinted Dodge pickup truck, still very angry as he headed to one of his other secret stash spots. King got out of the truck and walked inside of the house, slamming the door behind him. He took down a large mirror hanging on the living room wall. He put the combination into the safe, opened it up, and grabbed six ten thousand dollar stacks. He put them inside of a shoe box and walked outside of the house.

He was still spending money he stashed from two years ago, so sixty racks was nothing to him! He called all of his affiliates, his closest of family, and went to the house where he was keeping David's daughter.

She was beautiful with hazel eyes like her mother's, brown skin with a bit of vanilla, and long, curly brown hair. She looked just like David, having the same nose, eyes, and, most of all, the eye brows. King looked over Devunyae one last time as a tear trickled down the face of a soldier. He walked her to the car sad that he was giving her back. Over years of being in her life, treating her as if she was his own, he developed feelings for her.

They headed off to meet with a few of his soldiers at the Seventeenth Street Diner in Harrisburg. He parked his truck and got into his partner's car. They were all in there loading up their guns.

"Nah, my G. This time it's different. Just watch my back. This nicca got my mom and my daughter. He already killed my sister, man. I can't lose my mom and my daughter. I'm-a catch his ass on the rebound. Chess over checkers, my nicca," King said.

King picked up the phone and called his mother's phone back. David picked it up.

"Meet me at Double D's parking lot in the back by the dumpsters. If I see anybody else with you, kiss your mother goodbye. I have your princess with me now, so meet me there in twenty minutes. Give the money and my daughter to my homie and then he will give you your daughter. If you follow the instructions I am giving you, then I will tell you where your mother is." David said.

"Motherfucker, you know this will never be over. I'm going to catch you on the rebound and snatch your heart from out of your chest. I got killers that got killers all around the world, nicca. The hit gone be so big on your head that the president will take it!" King said.

"Is that right? I'm going to be waiting, so don't take too long, motherfucker. Remember this: I know where you at, your family that you love so dearly. I'm a ghost, bra. Like you said, you can't kill what's already dead," David spat back.

Ten minutes passed and David was parked at the gas station on Nineteenth and Paxton Street. He was waiting for King to call and say he was there. The phone rang and David picked it up. "You there, nicca?"

"Yeah, I'm here, pussy."

"There's been a change of plans. Pull off and follow the black truck that's parked there. When you get to the destination at hand, get out of your car and hop inside the cab that's there waiting for you. Stay in the cab and your daughter will come get my daughter and the money. Tell Spirit to take my daughter and the money back to the black truck. Once she hands over everything to my folks, she will be released over to you. I only tell you once that I have zero tolerance for that funny, clown, comedian shit. Try and play with me, bra. The beam on her back at all times," David said.

"Nah, I'm-a give you the money first. Then when you give me my mother, you get your daughter," King said.

"Pussy, this isn't negotiable. Follow my commands or your daughter and your mom dies. To be honest, I never met my daughter. She only two years old, dog. I can have five more of those, you hear me?" David asked.

King's daughter got out of the truck shivering, crying, and walking toward the cab. She grabbed the bag of money and David's daughter from King. She walked it over to the black truck and handed it to Danny. He looked through it, making sure it was all there and real. He told her to wait as he alerted David that he had Devunyae and the money. David gave permission for Spirit to be released into her father's arms. She ran to her father, crying as he held her tightly, making sure that she was okay.

The anger on King's face was very noticeable. He'd never been defeated in war, never been so humiliated. He tried to call his mother's phone to ask David where she was, but it went straight to voicemail. His whole body tensed up, praying that she was okay, hoping David didn't do the unthinkable. He called and called, but it still went to voicemail. The black truck vanished and he had no way to contact David. King was devastated, knowing he was outsmarted and lost his mother and sister for it. He cried and cried, knowing he could never call the police. King was silenced, defeated, crying and sobbing and showing a sensitive side no one had ever seen before. David had nothing to lose, no family, a foster child that would kill for nothing. His stomach turned upside down releasing his last meal on the side of the curb. He didn't know what to do or what direction to take; he would never forgive himself if he allowed his family to be murdered in vain.

The cab pulled off and King told the driver to drive, him and his daughter hand in hand, both still emotional. It'd been thirty minutes and King still hadn't talked to his mom or heard anything from David. He knew deep down that she was dead and there was nothing he could do about it. He took the cab back to his car, took his daughter to his aunt's house, and called his team up. When he got to his aunt's house, he couldn't tell her that her sister has been murdered. The only thing he could say was, "Auntie, watch her for a minute for me, I'm-a be right back." As he walked out the door, his phone started ringing. The number was blocked.

"Oh, bitch ass nicca, you sounding all pussy and scared. I thought you was a gangster? I told your old ass you could never outsmart me. I live this life, bra! I had your family in my hands—I could've killed them all. You don't want these problems, hoe ass nicca. I haven't touched your mother, she's good. Your mother's safely at home, stop crying, bitch," David said with a laugh, hanging up the phone.

King knew David would hit the sunset and vanish into thin air. He thought the war was over; deep inside he had no choice but to except his loss. He would remember David for the rest of his life. All King could do was hope, pray, and wish that he'd catch David on the rebound in this life or the next, then seek his revenge!

CHAPTER 36

HEAD OF SNAKE

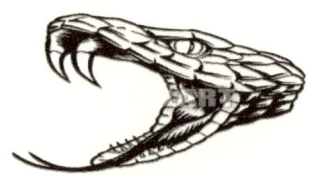

Eye of the cobra

David entered the back of his truck, sitting down next to his beautiful daughter, and stared at her with admiration. The day he'd been waiting for had finally arrived! After two years of worrying and suffering if his princess was alive and well, she was finally in David's care. He couldn't believe it was true; this heroic moment appeared daily in his dreams. Taking his daughter back from his enemy was a thirst that had to be quenched.

His eyes became watery and tears trickled down the sides of his cheeks. When he first laid eyes on her it was electrifying! It was like staring at his dead love, Danielle. She looked much like him, but had many of her mother's features. She was adorable, beautiful, sharing the same eye color and skin tone of Danielle.

1

David reached out, wanting to hold her and give her a hug. His daughter started kicking, screaming, and yelling at the top of her lungs, trying to get away. She cried for her so called father, King. She was terrified, as if he was a ghost that haunted her very dreams.

"I want my Dad, I want my Dad."

David started boiling like a pot of chicken grease. That was the last straw. David thought, *I'm-a blow this motherfuckers head off, I swear to God!* David was angry, his heart full of hurt that his princess loved his worst enemy. He wished he'd killed King's mother, daughter, and him when he had the chance! He couldn't live knowing that his enemy was still alive. When King said he'd send killers for him until his dying bed, it struck a chord through his body. King was very powerful, having allies across America, and with the internet he could send pictures of David across the world. David was too smart to allow himself to be in an uncompromising situation. If there was one thing he comprehended and understood, it was that the head of the snake must be decapitated!

David and his daughter arrived back at the hotel. Poca was there impatiently waiting and praying that everything went smoothly. After everything she'd been through in her life, the last thing she needed was another loss. David's daughter was still crying, still afraid, and not happy at all. David grabbed the plastic key out of his pocket and opened up the door. Poca ran up to David, giving him a hug and kiss, happy that he was back with his daughter.

"Papi, she is so beautiful. Oh my god, David, she looks just like you."

"I know, right? That's my little angel. Baby, come here. Let me holler at you real quick."

David grabbed her by the hand and walked her inside of the bathroom. Poca could tell by the look on David's face and the tears in his eyes that something was wrong. She didn't know what to think or what to expect, figuring since he had his daughter back he should be overjoyed.

"Papi, what's the matter? Why are you crying?" Poca asked.

"She is fucking scared of me. She thinks that King is her father. I can't believe this shit!"

"Well what did you expect, babe? She's three years old now and he's been raising her since she was a baby. She'll eventually come around and know you as her father. She just needs a little time," Poca said.

"Yeah, I feel you. That makes sense. But, baby, that shit hurts. I hate that motherfucker with a passion, and by all means necessary I'm-a smoke his ass! I'm-a cut the head of the snake and finish this war once and for all! I can't live with the fact, knowing one day, he could come back with no mercy and kill me. Look, I want you to take my daughter down to Philly and buy her some nice things. Poca, you left my side before, you're the last person I can trust. I need you now more than ever. If something happens to me, take

295

my daughter with you. We came up on at least a one hundred g's, so my money situation is straight."

"Papi, why don't we just leave while we have the chance? We can take the money and go anywhere. I'm tired of all this dick measuring, macho man shit," Poca said. "We can go to South America, Miami, Canada, wherever we want. Don't be stupid, Papi."

"I can't live like a pig or a coward, ducking and hiding from this motherfucker the rest of my life. He kidnapped my daughter. He has to die."

The fight had been won, but the war was still alive and wouldn't be over until King was terminated. When David spoke, his words stung her heart, reminding her so much of her brother. She knew there was no changing his mind.

She kissed him on the cheek. "Please be safe and come back to me. We need you."

David knew what he had to do, and he already knew where King was residing. David left the hotel room on his way to King's house on Division Street. He had one thing, and one thing only, on his mind and that was executing King. David was on his way to uptown Harrisburg taking the back roads and cut streets, so he'd avoid being spotted. He stopped at a stop sign and a Police K-9 truck pulled up in back of him. David's heart started racing, his mind thinking about if he should go on a high speed chase or shoot it out with the police.

David pulled off to the side of the road, remaining cool and trying not to make any sudden moves. The cops put on their sirens inches away from David's back bumper. Right as David was getting ready to murk off, the cops drove around him and made a left turn down Logan Street. David wiped off his forehead and continued driving to his desired location.

It had been a day since King had his mother and daughter back. His whole family was mourning the death of his sister, saddened due to the tragedy. The detectives and forensics were there asking everyone questions to see what was going on.

Detective Carter was the main detective assigned to all the murder cases in the 717 area. Carter knew about the war between King and David, knowing David was released from State Prison. He had a slight idea of who could've been behind King's sister's and boyfriend's murder. Carter was already angry, bitter that David beat all of the previous murder charges. He was at the point where he was ready to kill David himself, before any other innocent people died. King would never rat or give the cops any information or leads. He wanted David's life, his soul, and his bones to be buried six feet below the concrete.

King set a meeting up with his allies at a secret location. His out-of-state affiliates had already heard of the troubles King endured. They flew in from all over to be at his side. It was like the Black Mafia, even his Dominican connects in Philly came for support. King gave all of them pictures of David with the command that he wanted him alive, needing to kill David himself!

He put a 100,000 dollar price tag on his head, making sure that no one would be able to resist the offer.

They all stood there staring, quiet, and ready to seek revenge for their brother who lost his only sister. King wiped the tears from his eyes and squatted down low to the earth. He grabbed a hand full of dirt, the same dirt that his dead sister and Smooth laid upon. "This is what this man did to me and my family, my brother, my sister, and kidnapped my very own mother."

King stood up and released the dirt from his hands, throwing it into the air and walking away. Everyone walked to their cars with a picture of David. They all left on a mission trying to be the first one to get the money by bringing David to King. With little information, and having only a picture, they knew it'd be difficult.

Imagine trying to find a ghost—David was TTG, "trained to go," and good at being invisible! King had only a forty-eight hour window to find David, thinking, *this fuck nicca gone take the money and vanish into thin air.* Not once thinking that he was still in the area and planning a sneak attack.

Frustrated, he drove to his house on Division Street, trying to gather his thoughts. He was saddened that he put his family in this situation. His only sister was murdered by the same person who killed his best friend, Smooth. He started searching through the basket, looking for a card, so he could line his powder up. King rolled a twenty dollar bill and started snorting the lines of powder. He was kind of like Tony Montana in the movie *Scarface*. King laid on his couch and began thinking. He was slowly beginning to drift off into a light slumber at midnight in the silent house.

King turned all of his phones off, not wanting to trap or be bothered—he was in need of self-rest. He watched TV lying on the couch with his hands behind his head. He flicked through the channels trying to find something to watch. Eventually, the television started watching him while he slept on the intelligence of his enemy.

David was two steps ahead of him, already lamping in the back of King's house. David knew King would never let this war go until one of them was dead. David thought, *I got to kill this motherfucker before he gets to me.*

It was now or never. While everyone was out looking for him, he would be right under their nose waiting to strike like a cobra. He didn't want the detectives lurking around, not knowing if they knew of King's house on Division Street. If so, then it would be impossible to hit him quietly—it would most likely end in a bloody shootout. King was way too big for a fist fight; he had to put a bullet in his big ass.

David was hid, camouflaged in King's back yard behind some tall green bushes. He waited patiently for the perfect time to strike. He wanted to make sure there was no one else inside of the house. Coming from behind the bushes, he started climbing up the rail of the back porch. He was an excellent climber, monkey style, from when Smooth used to have him breaking into trap houses. He climbed to the second floor, with a book bag over his shoulder, blending in with the darkness of the night. David made it to the balcony and found himself staring into an empty room. He took off his book bag and took out a small red towel and a container full of lighter fluid. He put them in his back pocket, quietly took the air conditioner out of the window, and climbed inside.

He looked side to side, tiptoeing through the second floor. Once he heard the TV on downstairs in the living room, he figured that King was down there. David wanted to make a smooth getaway, leaving no traces and no leads back to him. As he tiptoed down the steps, he saw King laying on the couch fast sleep. David smiled as he got closer to the bottom step. He pulled his gun out and walked toward him. With a gloved hand, he grabbed the remote to the TV and turned it up.

King started moving, realizing the TV was too loud, and awakened from a much needed rest. When he woke up, he was face to face with a man in all black, with a Jason Voorhees mask over his face. David raised the gun and pointed it at him. He held the grip of the gun tightly and took off the mask. He wanted King to know who his killer was, making sure he remembered his face whenever they would meet at the cross roads.

"What's up now, Patna? You put a hit out on me, kidnapped my daughter, and raised her like she was yours, motherfucker! Look at your big ass lunching, sleeping? What, you thought I was going to let you live?"

King laid there in silence with his gun beneath the couch. David already had his weapon drawn, so it would be impossible to reach it. King knew this would be his last night, last breath, and last day on this earth. He wasn't scared to die—he knew one day his time would be up, bracing himself for the inevitable. So as David stood there with his gun pointed at him, he sat up and snorted another line of coke.

"Pussy, what you waiting for? If you think I'm begging for my life, you got me fucked up. Fuck you, bra. I'll be waiting for you in hell. See you when you get there, motherfucker!"

David stood there ready to pull the trigger, staring deeper into the eyes of the man he was getting ready to execute. "How you want it? Open or closed casket? Your choice."

"Fuck you, nicca. Suck my dick." And he hawk spit in David's face.

David wiped the spit off of his face with the bottom of his shirt and snapped. He took the gun and started bashing King in the head with it, swinging with all of his might, crushing the bones in his face and skull. King was already dead for at least two minutes while David continued pounding in his face with the gun. He wanted to make sure there would be no open casket. Every time he swung the gun, he thought of everything he'd been through. He heard the bones in his face and skull cracking, as blood splattered everywhere.

When David was finished, Kind was unrecognizable. David took the cloth from out of his back pocket and started cleaning the blood off of the gun. His clothes dripped with blood from King's fluids splashing him. He had an extra set of clothes, a sweat suit, and a pair of running shoes in his book bag just in case.

He opened the container of lighter fluid and started squirting it on King and everything else in the house. He had five packs of matches, planning to spark all of them starting from the first floor. David changed his bloody clothes, throwing them over top of King's body. He poured the rest of the lighter fluid on King and lit two matches and watched as King's body erupted into flames. The fire grew fast, and the pictures, the couches all burning and beginning to melt. The smoke grew thicker and thicker every second. It was getting harder for David to breathe. He coughed, choking on the smog.

He put his mask back on and ran up the steps. He started squirting the rest of the lighter fluid throughout the house, lighting a few more matches. David left just in time as the fire was closing in upon him. He left the same way he came in, out the window and down the balcony. He made it to the alleyway smiling, happy, as the house of his worst enemy was reduced to ashes. David walked away as if nothing ever happened. He was relieved that he single handedly cut the head off the snake.

David headed back to the hotel to see his daughter and Poca. He was paranoid the whole drive, praying he made it back to them safely. He pulled up to the condo smiling, relieved to know he completed the mission. He parked the car and started toward his condo. There was a drunken couple in front of the soda machine arguing. They were both highly upset and staggering from alcohol. The woman smacked the man on the side of his face and stormed away. David minded his own business and continued walking toward his room.

Poca and his daughter were already starting to build a bond. Poca was telling her silly jokes while combing and brushing her hair. David smiled and took off his shoes, lying down on the couch

"Papi, is everything okay?"

"All you need to know, ma, is that I am the realest nicca you ever met. Roll up some of that sour diesel. I need to get high," David said with a smirk.

"So can we leave this place and move on with our lives now? David, If you had one choice, if you could go anywhere in the world, where would you go?" Poca asked.

"I'm trying to go to South America and meet the source, one of them island boy connects," David said jokingly. "Psych, I'm fucking with you, babe. But I do want to move somewhere where it's sunny all year around."

"Rio de Janeiro," Poca shouted out like a school girl.

"I think I like how that sounds, baby. We could open up a little cabaña out on the beach or something."

"So let me ask you, are we still going to live that life or are we finished? Papi, you know me, anywhere I go my hustle ambitions will kick in. My money straight, but I can't live off that forever. So I'm with it, babe. Let's go find that connect you always dreamed about," Poca said.

"Whenever you ready, me, you, the baby, and Danny can go. I got my money right, yours is right. Let's go enjoy the rest of our lives!"

David wrapped Poca in his powerful, monstrous arms, hugging her as if he would never see her again. They both were high and in deep thought of their future together. They both had been through hell and back, with love and losses that clouded their mind while freezing their souls. All they could do was smile and laugh, knowing it had to be the Lord who delivered them to their freedom.

David accomplished his mission and cut the head off the snake. He missed his brother Smooth and Danielle, wondering if they were staring down at him. David was now mentally prepared to accept his faith— he was a dead man walking and there was nothing he could do about it. He vowed to live out his life free as long as God allowed him to see another day.

Poca laid her head on his shoulder and they drifted off to sleep. David's daughter watched them closely, confused of her new beginning. The real

Bonnie and Clyde were back together, stronger than ever. They woke up with their eyes to the future and not the past!

"False Realities Expressed Every day."

F.R.E.E

False Realities Expressed Every Day

David lived his life like a chess game, always thinking three steps ahead. He was a strategic male using people as ponds for higher leverage. He was an author of his life and every page, every chapter was filled with loneliness. David accepted his faith, and embraced his karma as it came back in full throttle. He understood his position in life as a tyrant, pirate, and a murderer. Through all the bloodshed and innocent lives that were taken by his hands, all he ever wanted was a family, a home, and to be loved. When your feet are deep in the mud, it's like trying to get out of quick sand. They say to follow the rainbow and there's a shiny pot of gold. They never tell you about the curse, the Leprechauns waiting to take your soul!

Written by Preston A. Dent

PRESTON W/ DAVID BILLBOARD

PRESTON AT PA NEWS STATION

LESEAN MCCOY

RASHEEDA LOVE AND HIP HOP

LENNY SANTIAGO AT ROC NATION

STEVIE J.

Does this book touch you?

Would you love to see this book as a movie?

Let Preston Know.

- Read Preston's Famous Author reviews

- Watch Preston's interviews, commercials, and book trailers.

- Look at Preston's photo gallery with celebrities

- Preston's next book signing, film festival and events.

- Purchase Preston's latest novels!